MW00325537

LESBIAN COWBOYS

LESBIAN COWBOYS

EROTIC ADVENTURES

EDITED BY
SACCHI GREEN & RAKELLE VALENCIA

CLEIS
PRESS

Copyright © 2009 by Sacchi Green & Rakelle Valencia.

All rights reserved. Except for brief passages quoted in newspaper, magazine, radio, or television reviews, no part of this book may be reproduced in any form or by any means, electronic or mechanical, including photocopying or recording, or by information storage or retrieval system, without permission in writing from the publisher.

Published in the United States by Cleis Press Inc., P.O. Box 14697, San Francisco, California 94114.

Printed in Canada.
Cover photograph: Kimball Hall/Photodisc
Cover design: Scott Idleman
Text design: Frank Wiedemann
Cleis Press logo art: Juana Alicia
First Edition.
10 9 8 7 6 5 4 3 2 1

ISBN 13: 978-1-57344-361-6

Contents

| INTRODUCTION

"Cowboy" is a calling, a vocation, not a gender, and some of the toughest cowboys aren't boys at all. The life is rough and gritty, as much down to earth as tall in the saddle. The lesbian cowboys in these stories work hard, play hard, and love hard, in the Old West, New West, or anywhere in the world. Above all, they ride hard, whether on a horse or a woman.

"Cowboy" is also a legend, an attitude, and a state of mind. These women do the work and walk the walk. They know what they want and take it, and give back as good as they get. For all their similarities, each is a distinct individual, with stories that vary from profoundly moving to gripping to as edgy as shiny spurs. The settings cover a wide range as well, from Australia to New England to the Great Plains and the Rockies, and from the wildest days of the west through two World Wars to right now.

In contemporary stories, Radclyffe and Jove Belle give us very different views of riders who hold their own in the limelight of the rodeo, and then hold a woman close to ease their aches and loneliness and tension. Jean Roberta and Elazarus Wills follow loners running away from themselves until older and wiser lovers set them back on track. Cheyenne Blue shows the conflict between traditional cattle ranching and the new environmentalism in Australia, when sparks fly between opponents. Rakelle Valencia and Sacchi Green portray very different equine specialists, one a farrier and one a pulling-horse competitor, driven to the edge by extreme desires. Roxy Katt injects humor into role-playing, while DeJay brings heat and tenderness to a tale of longtime lovers. Delilah Devlin's "The Hired Hand" is every inch a woman and more than a match for any man.

Some of the action is set in historical periods when the only way for some women to be themselves was to pass as men. Andrea Dale's poker player has to do it long enough to win that all-important pot; Teresa Wymore's Pinkerton detective takes on the lifelong role with gusto; and Cecilia Tan's young ranch hand survives an initiation in an old-west bordello to prove that she's "Man Enough." In a later era, during World War II, Craig J. Sorensen's young rebel proves her ability to run the ranch as well or better than any man when her brothers are lost in battle, while Charlotte Dare's drifter keeps searching for somewhere to live out an identity that matters more even than love.

Ride along with us on these fifteen erotic adventures of lust, dust and leather, ropes and saddles, with lesbian cowboys vivid enough to be real and sexy enough to fantasize about. If you work up a sweat, and we sure hope you do, come right on down to the bunkhouse and join us. There's plenty of steam in the shower, and the loving is hot anywhere you look.

FREEDOM RIDES

Radclyffe

At least they didn't bring her in on a stretcher this time. She walked into the emergency medical tent under her own power, looking moderately embarrassed. This was the third time in five weeks I'd seen her—well, professionally at least. I saw her around the rodeo circuit far more often than that, especially since I was looking for her. I doubt that she even remembered me. The first time we'd met, I buddy-taped her broken finger. The second time, a month ago, she'd been kicked in the head by an out-of-control steer and she couldn't even remember her own name. This time, she had a nasty scrape over the arch of her left cheekbone. From what I could see beneath the sweat-streaked dust that caked her skin, it didn't look too bad. I sighed inwardly in relief and shook my head.

"I've seen you ride and I've seen you rope, so I know you're good. But you're definitely an accident magnet."

She grinned and her face flushed, making her look unexpectedly young. She wasn't, as I knew from having scanned her vital statistics the last time she'd come in for treatment. She was about my age, early thirties. Her thick, collar-length sun-bleached hair, clear blue eyes, and smooth skin might have made her look delicate if she weren't so lean and muscled, and if she didn't have a year-round tan and fine squint lines around her eyes and at the corners of her mouth that said she spent all her time outdoors under the merciless sun doing hard work.

The first time I saw her ride in with the rodeo crowd, I wondered what made a woman choose such a hard life. Physically strenuous, often dangerous, and probably lonely. I mean, I worked mostly with men, too, but I didn't eat and sleep with them for a good part of the year. Out here in west Texas, the rodeo circuit lasted longer than most other places, and I worked a lot of the events since I'd never really settled into a regular medical practice. I guess that made the two of us a little alike— we were both itinerants in our own way.

"What happened?" I asked, indicating a stool next to the counter where I kept most of the first-aid supplies. I had a crash cart, which thankfully I almost never had to use, with drugs, a defibrillator, and even an airway. In my two seasons staffing the medical tent, the most serious illness I'd had to treat was a heart attack. Fortunately, he stabilized right away with oxygen and nitroglycerin. Broken bones didn't count. They were routine on the circuit.

"I got a little too close to the rail trying to pick up a rider thrown by a bronc," she said, sounding more disgusted than concerned.

I pulled over a portable light on a swivel arm, shined it onto the side of her face, and gently swabbed the area with saline-soaked gauze. "Well, you've got splinters in your cheek." They looked nasty, and I knew it had to hurt, but she seemed completely unfazed. I turned away, appalled that my hands were shaking. We were alone in the tent, and I could hear the crowd in the distance cheering. "I'm going to need to anesthetize the area with some local so I can get them out. Are you allergic to any medications?"

"No. But you don't need the local. Just go ahead and do what you need to do."

I spun back, hands on hips. "There's no one watching. You don't need to be tough in here."

She laughed, clearly amused. "I'm not trying to be. But I've been banged around, broken, and bruised most of my life. A few little pieces of wood aren't going to bother me."

"Well, they're going to bother me," I muttered. Over her protests, I injected the area, plucked out the slivers, and then coated the area with antibiotic ointment. "Keep it clean—"

She laughed again, and I couldn't help but join her. "All right. Wash it frequently, then, and reapply the ointment."

"I will. Thanks." As she rose from the stool, she winced.

"Wait a minute," I said. "What else is wrong?"

"Just a bruise," she said.

I'd been so captivated by her face, and worried about the abrasion, I hadn't noticed that the left shoulder of her shirt was torn, and now that I looked more closely, caked with blood. "Stay put. What else happened?"

She shook her head, looking confused. "I told you. I hit a rail."

"You didn't tell me you'd been crushed into the fence." I tried not to shout at her, but I was worried. And embarrassed that I hadn't done a proper evaluation because I'd been thinking about how attractive she was. I'd been thinking *that* since the first day I saw her ride in. I've never seen a woman look so good in dusty jeans, scuffed boots, and a sweat-soaked shirt. She just seemed so damn comfortable in her skin, and so sure of herself.

And I'll admit, she looked sexy on that horse, her ass lifting and her crotch rocking in the saddle, her strong thighs bunching rhythmically. I had an instantaneous image of me underneath her, her lean thighs straddling my hips, her wet sex rolling and thrusting into mine.

What is it that makes cowboys so sexy, anyhow? I thought to myself, motioning her back down on the stool.

"It's all a fantasy," she said. "Nothing glamorous about scrapes and blisters and bruises."

I closed my eyes for a second, unable to believe I'd actually said that out loud. "I am so sorry."

She grinned. "I'm not. I mean, if you think I'm sexy."

"Pretend I didn't say that. I need you to take off your shirt." I looked her square in the eyes when I said it, because I had to get the conversation back on professional grounds. Lord, her eyes were blue. As blue as an August afternoon. And as I stared into them, they darkened and I felt my heart rate soar.

Still looking into my eyes, she slowly unbuttoned her shirt. It took every ounce of my willpower not to look down as she shrugged it off and tossed it onto the counter across from us. I finally managed to break away from her mesmerizing gaze and slipped around behind her. She wore a sleeveless T-shirt underneath the denim shirt she'd just removed. "I'm going to lift this up. You've got another scrape over your shoulder and down your back."

"I'll take it off."

"Let me help you." My fingers were trembling as I carefully tugged the thin, ribbed cotton from the waistband of her jeans. When she lifted her arms, the muscles in her shoulders and back stood out in stark relief. Her back was beautiful, sculpted and honed from hard labor. I was careful not to touch her as I lifted her shirt over her arms and laid it aside. "You've got a lot of superficial scratches. They need to be cleaned. Do you have a shower in your trailer?"

"No. We're using the public ones down the road while we're here. They're closed until six tomorrow morning."

"Well, this can't wait." I picked up the two-way radio and called my backup. He was somewhere in the stands watching the events. "Don, I have to leave for a while. Can you come back and cover for me? Thanks."

"Slip this back on." I held out her shirt. "We've got a decontamination shower in our van. Let's get you cleaned up."

"It's really nothing."

"It really is." She wasn't badly hurt and didn't need my assistance in any real professional capacity any longer, but she did need to have that shoulder washed. The moment I stopped feeling like she was a patient, my gaze drifted down to her breasts. They were exactly as I imagined they would be. Small, round, and high with tight pink nipples perfectly centered. Her chest muscles were broad and full, accentuating the soft, nearly incongruous curves of her breasts. Her abdominals were cut, the skin stretched taut over the washboard abs, something I'd only ever seen once before, on a female rower. Her waist tapered to narrow hips and long thighs. A faint line of golden hair ran from her navel downward and disappeared beneath the waistband of her jeans. She was the perfect icon of female strength, and I was instantly, utterly, shamelessly aroused. When I looked up, her eyes were hooded, her lips turned up slightly at the corners. She knew.

"Come on," I said hoarsely. "I'll take you to the trailer."

Watching me, knowing I was watching her, she didn't button her shirt, but only tucked the tails into her jeans, leaving a deep open vee from her neck to the base of her torso. I desperately wanted to skim my fingers down that bare expanse of flawless skin, so I turned my back and walked away. I heard her boots scuff the ground behind me an instant before I felt her fingers at the small of my back. Her breath was warm against my neck.

"You won't get in any sort of trouble, will you?" she asked.

"No," I said. Not the kind of trouble she was thinking of. I was already in far more trouble than I'd ever imagined. I unlocked the trailer and pulled the shades on the small windows on either side of the door before turning on the light. "It's back this way."

I led her down the narrow aisle between the lockers holding our emergency supplies to the compartment at the rear that housed a sink and shower stall. There was barely room for two people to turn around in it. I stepped in first and set the temperature gauge on the thermal unit that heated the water. "It will only take a few minutes for this to warm. Why don't you get undressed…"

When I turned back, the words died in my throat. She was bare-chested again and her jeans were open and halfway down her hips. The golden triangle between her thighs was visible in the open fly of her dusty blue jeans. "Oh, God."

"I was hoping you would stay," she said softly, and her bravery undid me.

"What makes a woman want to be a cowboy?" I whispered, skimming my fingers through her hair. If I leaned forward just a little, my breasts would touch hers. At the thought, my nipples tightened painfully.

"I didn't know I wanted to be a cowboy, not at first." She kicked off her boots and pushed her jeans down. When she stepped out of them, she was naked. "I only knew I wanted to be free."

"Are you?"

"Mostly." She cupped my jaw and kissed me.

The palm of her hand was rough in places, incredibly soft in others. Her mouth tasted like an endless summer afternoon, shimmering with heat and sultry air. She teased inside my mouth with the tip of her tongue and I sucked on it, wanting more. Wanting her deeper. I slid my fingers into her hair and pressed closer.

"I don't want to hurt your face," I gasped. "Your back."

She laughed. "I've been run down, kicked, and trampled and climbed back into the saddle. I'm just fine."

As if to prove it to me, she wrapped her arms around my waist, lifted me up, and took two steps forward. I yelped when warm water cascaded over me, clothes and all. She reached behind her and pulled the narrow glass door closed, and then pressed me against the nearest wall. Her lips danced along my jaw, her teeth scraping lightly down my neck. I arched my back, tilting my pelvis into hers.

"God, I've got to get these clothes off," I gasped. "I want your skin."

She made a noise deep in her throat, more a growl than a groan, and then she was tugging at my scrub shirt and I was fumbling with the zipper on my jeans. With the bottom of my shirt bunched in her hands, she tugged it up and I raised my arms so she could get it off. Desperately, I shimmied my hips and forced the heavy wet denim down my thighs. I toed off my sneakers and kicked everything away from me. In a flash her thigh was between mine and her weight was against me, pinning me to the shower wall. I dug my fingers into her back, low down above the hard rise of her ass, and rode her thigh, rolling my sex over the hard muscle until I was open and my bare clitoris rubbed along her skin. She sucked on my neck just below my ear, her hands kneading my breasts and squeezing my nipples. With each pluck of her fingers on my nipples she pumped her crotch into me. My clit tightened and twitched. Fire scorched my belly, a red-hot blaze sending sparks into the midnight sky.

"I am going to come all over you," I warned breathlessly.

"Yes, you are," she murmured, her lips roaming over my ear. "You're gonna spill all that sweetness just for me." Shifting a little, she slid her hand between us and gripped my whole sex in her hand, forcing my clit back beneath the hood, holding off my orgasm. Then her tongue was in my mouth again and she was massaging me, rhythmically squeezing the length of my clitoris between the folds of my own swollen flesh.

Aching to come, I gripped her ass and attacked her tongue, sucking and tugging on it. Her thighs trembled against mine and a rush of hot slickness coated my leg. She was close to coming. I whimpered as her thumb pressed the base of my clitoris and worked the distended shaft in short hard circles against my pubic bone. Still she kept my sex clamped in her fist. I jerked my mouth away from hers.

"Let me come, damn you."

Her eyes were nearly closed, her chest heaving as her hips pistoned, grinding her sex into me. Out of nowhere, I pictured her riding onto the grounds again, her thighs clenching and relaxing, her pelvis lifting and falling. So strong, so proud, so utterly beautiful.

"Wait," I exclaimed, pushing her away with more strength than I thought I had. I dropped to my knees. "I want you to ride my face until you come in my mouth."

She thrust her arms straight out against the wall and spread her legs, pushing herself toward my mouth. "Hurry. Suck my clit. Hurry."

I spread her open with my thumbs, and the water streamed down the hard planes of her belly around the up-thrust prominence of her deep red clit. She was so swollen the hood had retracted, and I closed my lips around the smooth, firm head and sucked. She cried out and her hips heaved. I kept her open with one hand and wrapped the other arm around her, holding her against my mouth. Her clit was already pulsing with the first surge of orgasm, but I wasn't going to let her off with a short ride. She was going to go until the buzzer. I felt her come against my lips and never stopped swirling my tongue around her, sucking her, shaking my head from side to side with her clit in my mouth.

"You're gonna make me come again," she muttered, her voice barbed-wire tight.

I murmured *yes* and milked her clit with my lips and she came on me, in me. I spread my legs as she slumped to her knees; then I was straddling her, my clit against her stomach, rubbing, rubbing, working myself over those hard abs. Oh, so close.

"I want to come so bad," I whimpered, barely remembering not to clutch onto her injured shoulder. I cupped my own breasts instead, twisting my nipples to make my clit tingle and go off. Pressure built in my clit and spread into my belly and down my legs. Not long now. Not long. I grabbed for my clit to finish it, and she brushed my hand aside. Her fingers closed on me and I looked down, my vision blurring, and saw her long, work-roughened fingers rolling and pulling my clit. Then her other hand was there, filling me. Too much. Too good. I came all over her hands.

"Sweet," she murmured. "So fucking sweet."

I didn't say anything, I couldn't. I just curled up in her arms while the warm water rolled over us. After a few minutes, we staggered out and I found a towel and gently dried her face.

"I need to put some more ointment on these scrapes," I said, my voice sounding huskier than normal. "I want you to know I've never done anything quite like this, and I don't believe I've ever come so hard."

"I like the sounds of the last part." She grinned and kissed me.

"Turn around. I want to see your back." As I carefully blotted the skin around the large abrasion, I said as casually as I could, "You'll be moving on to the next town on the circuit soon, won't you."

She looked over her shoulder at me, her eyes going midnight again. "One of the best parts about being free is you don't have to leave to prove it."

"Well," I said, trailing my fingers over her mouth, "I hope you feel free to come back anytime then."

When she kissed me, I knew she'd be back, and I finally understood what was so damn sexy about cowboys. When they came to you, for you, the ride was like no other.

QUEENS UP

Andrea Dale

It was my daddy who taught me to play poker.

He was a good father as fathers go, I suppose, especially considering my mother died when I was four and he had his hands full raising me. He was also a very good teacher, and I was hustling the ranch hands before some of them realized the ragged moppet who dogged their heels was not, in fact, of the male persuasion. Took them a right long while, too, considering how I'd been so modest about peeing in front of 'em.

I tended toward wearing men's clothes even as I grew older, because it was much easier roping cattle in breeches than a skirt, and skirts were just nuisances anyway, not to mention stockings and petticoats, and besides, there was no one around to properly lace me into a corset.

Even my childhood playmate Margaret Compton didn't know when we were children. Which is why when we grew older things grew a mite complicated, because I had a crush on her.

In the end, though, it worked out fine, because sweet Margaret

Compton wasn't about to go getting any crushes on men, either, and when she found out my secret, well, we then had a delicious secret to share, just between us two.

But I was talking about my daddy.

For all he was a good man at heart, the problem was simple. There was one other thing that he was good at, and that was drinking. So, for all his good teaching of the cards, my father wasn't a very good poker *player* at all.

Which is how he came to lose our family's ranch to one Mister Samuel Owens.

By the time this happened, I'd been running the ranch for years, not that anyone outside knew that. Wasn't proper for a woman to be making such decisions—what did a pretty thing know about cattle and budgets and weather patterns and ordering men around? So my daddy was the figurehead, the one who went to the bank and the auctions (on mornings after I'd hidden his bottles so his head would be clear). Me, I balanced the books and wrote up orders for supplies and, yes, bossed the men around, but by that time they knew I was capable and cared enough about the ranch to keep our secret safe.

God took pity on me the next morning when Samuel came out to the ranch to take a good, long look at his new ownings (not that I knew the reason for his visit as yet).

I wasn't riding out on the back forty or forking hay off a wagon that day. Instead, I was inside catching up on some business correspondence for my daddy to sign when he woke up from last night's binge, and Margaret had time to run in and let me know company was approaching.

I'd have to play hostess while someone roused Daddy and stuck his head under the pump to shock some soberness into him.

Margaret was more versed in the intricacies of women's clothing than I, so she rushed about gathering skirts and boots with tiny buttons and whatever else I'd need to shoehorn myself into.

At that point in our relationship, we had to keep things pretty quiet, so Margaret slept in the servants' quarters and our trysts were rare, stolen moments. Her own daddy had died coming up on two years ago, and I'd promised him that we'd take care of Margaret as if she were one of my own. And she was my own—she had my heart, and I hers. By outside appearances, she was our maid and cook, and when the occasional hand took a fancy to courting her, she smiled and gently eased his attentions aside.

My point being, when I looked up from shucking my shirt and trousers, I shouldn't have been surprised by the look in her eyes.

Hunger. Need. Lust.

The same sensations flared through me, ignited a fire in my belly—and below.

Aware of my own foolishness, I still couldn't help but step toward her, take her face in my hands, kiss her.

Every time I kissed her was heaven, but it had been far too long since we'd been able to be together, and so the sweet heat of her mouth was a desperate homecoming. I wanted to devour her, be devoured by her. Her tongue danced with mine, and all I could think of was how that tongue felt in the hollow of my shoulder, on the hard peak of my breast, at the juncture between my thighs.

I moaned, and she answered. I wound my fingers into the honey-colored upsweep of her soft hair and kissed her as if I were making love to her. Right now this was the only moment I had, and if I didn't have time to strip her and lay her down beside me and love her properly, I could at least do this.

But it couldn't be that way, and it couldn't go on forever.

Her whimper as I pulled away almost drove me to my knees, because her desperation and desire mirrored my own. I was hot and wet and quivering on the edge, and all I'd done was kiss her.

If her hands hadn't been full of my dress and petticoats and stockings—if she'd stroked between my legs—I would have known the oblivion I craved.

No time. I kissed her on the tip of her pert nose and whispered my love and apologies. One reason I love her is that she understands the tightrope I must walk.

It was excruciating to feel her hands on me and have them putting clothes on me, not stripping them off. Every tug that tightened my corset lacings was like a step closer to the gallows. How I ached to be naked in her arms, breasts pressed to breasts, fingertips chasing over skin and raising gooseflesh and desire.

Later. I promised us both that.

My father was being fetched, and Samuel Owens awaited me in the parlor.

"Why, Miss Josephine, you are quite a sight today," Samuel said, rising with his hat in his hand to greet me. Oh, he might have said the right words, acted all solicitous and proper, but his eyes revealed his true thoughts. His gaze raked over me, greedy and lascivious, a disgusting parody of the way Margaret had stared in awe at my figure just a few moments ago.

Oily, I thought. Oily Owens, that's what they called him behind his back, and I could see why.

"And a good day to you, Mr. Owens," I said, my smile as sweet as I could manage, and him no wiser for it. "What brings you out here this fine day?"

His eyebrows shot up. "Your daddy didn't tell you?"

Now I felt like *I'd* been sitting under the water pump. Oh, Daddy, what have you done?

"I haven't spoken to my father yet today," I said. "He's been…"

I couldn't say *indisposed,* because I guessed Samuel Owens had been witness to my daddy's drinking the night before.

"…occupied," I finished.

Samuel wasn't a good enough actor to suppress a snort of derision, although he seemed to catch himself enough to bite back whatever it was his first instinct to say.

"Well, now, I hope he's not too occupied to see me," he said. "We have some business to attend to, your father and I. You might want to fetch him, Miss Josephine, and hear what needs to be said, as it involves you."

At first I couldn't imagine what business Samuel might have with my father (since I knew firsthand what-all business was to be had regarding the workings of the ranch), much less how it could involve me.

But I'm not stupid, and a sick gnawing started in my chest that had nothing to do with the tightness of my corset.

When Daddy wouldn't meet my eye as we sat down at the kitchen table, I knew something was very, very wrong. Much worse than just another dreadful night at the card table.

"Jo—Josephine," Daddy said. "I had a run of bad luck with the cards last night…"

And I knew, with head-spinning certainty, what he'd done.

I would not—would *not*—faint like a simpering girl. No matter how hard it was to draw in a full breath in this damnable contraption.

"Now, Miss Josephine," Samuel broke in, "I'm not a hard-hearted man. I know we can come to an equitable agreement that keeps your family's ranch intact."

I was certain his heart was as hard as another part of him, given the way he couldn't keep his eyes off the swell of my breasts, but I held my tongue.

It came as no real surprise that the ranch wasn't really what Samuel had sought to win in that game. What my daddy had thoughtlessly tossed into the pot, believing his hand was the unbeatable one, was me. *My* hand—in marriage.

Well, of course I gathered what dignity I could and politely told Mr. Samuel Owens that we appreciated his offer greatly, but that my hand was not available at this time, and wasn't there some other way we could resolve this issue to our mutual satisfaction?

The fact to me was simple: No, there was not.

He went on speaking quietly, outwardly calm, but the way his face flushed and his hat shook in his hands made it clear he was reining in his anger.

Seeing as we were all in the middle of calving season, he said, he'd give me two weeks to think over his offer. At the end of those two weeks, if my answer was the same as it was now, then we would have three days to remove ourselves and our belongings from the premises, or Samuel would see to it that the sheriff did so.

Then he stood, jammed his hat back on his head, and walked out of the house, his footsteps slamming down on the floorboard of the porch as if he were marking the house as his own with his boot heels.

We did not have the money to buy the ranch back from Samuel.

We did not have anywhere to go, any real means of income, without the ranch.

Oh, we could go work on someone else's ranch—if I had to scrub floors, I was perfectly capable of doing so—but my father's health wouldn't allow for riding the range or baling hay, and I couldn't support him on a maid's salary.

There was whoring, of course, but if I was going to do that, I might as well marry Samuel and keep the ranch in the family.

My father, bless him, never said a word about that, never spoke once about that arrangement being the only thing that could save us. I saw it in his eyes, when he thought I wasn't looking. But he never said it aloud, and I loved him for that.

We were four days from our deadline, with no miracle in sight, and Margaret had been quietly packing up my mother's bone china when my father wasn't around (I had already been through her jewelry, estimating how much I could get for it and how long we could live on that money), when a chance—just a fleeting chance—presented itself.

One of the hands happened to mention the rumor of a poker game in Haldern City: A high-stakes game, with men coming from all over the territory to participate.

The type of game Samuel Owens wouldn't be able to pass up.

My plan was plumb crazy. I don't deny that for one second. Given what was at stake, though, crazy was all we had left.

I took a loan out against the ranch. Samuel had the deed in his hands, but hadn't told the bank that yet, and the banker was my mother's cousin once removed.

If I lost the game, I'd no doubt be seeing the next few years from the inside of a jail cell, but I had no choice.

My breasts were fortunately small; bound properly, they wouldn't be obvious. But Margaret still fretted, and I'd be lying if I said I didn't share her worries. Passing myself off as a boy when I was ten years old was different than trying it at twenty, even with a hat low over my brow and a fake mustache that in daylight looked like the runt of the litter had chosen my lip to expire on.

The only likely person to recognize me would be Samuel, who didn't know me in anything but flounces and bows.

The hardest part was my hair. Margaret wept as she sliced the scissors through it and the long black locks littered the floor. I hadn't thought I'd care, but the sight of my shorn head in the mirror was disturbing, unreal.

How I'd explain it away after the game was something I just didn't have time to concern myself with.

I was more worried that my father would want to go to Haldern City himself, but the loss of the ranch had broken his spirit. He had nothing left to gamble away.

The thing with plans is sometimes you get so caught up in them that you don't realize someone else is making plans, too.

My sweet, cunning Margaret intended to make sure no one suspected my name wasn't Joseph.

I'd been lying for so long to keep the ranch running that it came easily to me. Still, one gentleman kept asking, "Now, what parts did you say you were come from?"

I'd mentioned a city far enough away that none of them knew it well, but I still couldn't slip up on any details. Another muttered, "Awfully skinny looking fellow," to his acquaintance.

I knew my face was too smooth. I knew my voice hovered on the high side of tenor.

If I was found out, there was no telling what they'd do. All I knew is that I'd be in a world of hurt—if I made it out of there at all—and the ranch would be lost forever.

To say I was tense during the first hand was an understatement, which is why, even with the decent cards I had, I bowed out early. I needed to focus, to concentrate, and to gauge my opponents. My father had given me a few tips about Samuel (none of which I figured I could actually count on), but most of the men were unknown to me. Two more I knew from town, but not well enough to judge them now.

I could do this. All I had to do was read my cards, read my opponents, not get greedy. Focus on Samuel, push him until he had no choice but to ante up more than he ever planned to.

"Why, Joseph, there you are!"

I knew that voice. But it couldn't be...

Tarted up with rouge and paint, her curves cinched into a tiny corset, her breasts nearly spilling out over the low-cut ruffles, Margaret was near to unrecognizable to me. She'd dyed her hair a shocking red, and the beauty spot on her cheek looked as though she'd had it since she was a squalling babe.

I stole a quick glance at Samuel, frantically trying to recall if he'd ever met her and, if he had, would he be likely to remember her face.

But he was as mesmerized as the rest of them.

The rest of *us*, I should say, because I could barely keep my eyes off of her. She was beautiful in her gaudiness, no more beautiful than she always was to me, but in a different way now.

Her fearlessness and ingenuity had a lot to do with that.

The man who kept asking where I was from—Ed was his name—actually stood and touched his forehead. "Greetings, ma'am," he said, with that touch of irony all men have when greeting saloon girls, "and who might you be?"

Her laugh tinkled musically. "Why, I'm Joseph's good luck charm, or so he says. He never plays a game without me." She leaned forward, just a little, and the men all leaned forward, just a little, hoping for a glimpse of more secret flesh. "Now, if my presence is bothering you-all, I'd be happy to wait outside."

They swallowed, they twitched, they considered. It wasn't as if we didn't have other such girls in the room, freshening our drinks, singing a song or two. There was always the chance, though, that Margaret and I could have some sort of cheating scam set up.

Samuel, of all people, spoke first. "I say let her stay," he said. "She'll no doubt distract poor Joseph here more than any of us, and that's money in our pockets!"

The others whooped and agreed. They whooped even louder when Margaret bent over me and angled for a kiss, which I was more than happy to oblige.

She made my head spin and my skin shiver, and for a moment she was the entirety of my world. It was only the knowledge that I had to win back the ranch so that I could give her a home, a home with me, that pulled me back to the stink and sweat and clamor of the room.

Because they expected me to, I slapped her bottom lightly and told her to get me a whiskey. With a saucy grin, she asked if any of the other gentlemen needed a refilling of their refreshments, which caused the other girls to scowl when several of my opponents took Margaret up on her offer.

Ed dealt the next hand. It was hell focusing on the cards and not on Margaret's fine bottom. Thankfully I wasn't the only one who was distracted.

I felt a little bit more confident with this hand. I was getting to know the other players, and thanks to Margaret, I wasn't as worried at being found out.

Cards were examined. Odds were considered. Bets were made.

Margaret came back and distributed drinks. I took a cautious sip of mine—it would be too obvious if I completely ignored it. Oh, smart girl! She'd watered it down.

To solidify our relationship, and to the hoots and comments of the men, she settled down on my knee.

She smelled sweet—some sort of lavender powder she'd dusted on—and I knew she tasted even sweeter. And it'd been too long since I'd tasted that honeyed sweetness.

If I'd had male parts, I'd've been drilling through her petticoats right about now.

My thighs were sweaty and itchy in my woolen trousers, but my pearl was slick and throbbing. I couldn't resist letting my hand slide up the boning along Margaret's waist to rest on the curve of her breast. Beneath the ruffles, I knew I could find her sensitive peak. There was so much temptation to lose myself in her...but we both had to deny ourselves pleasure, and to struggle with arousal and desire.

No matter what the outcome of the game would be, I whispered her a promise: Tonight. Tonight would be ours.

My daddy always said that playing poker was a right bit more interesting than the telling of it afterwards. If the game had gone badly, I wouldn't be relating this tale.

Suffice to say I got Samuel Owens where I wanted him: Out of money, out of sense, and full of desperate pride. He threw the deed to my family's ranch into the pot with a comment about how the ranch wasn't as important to him as the prize he'd still get to keep. Margaret froze on my lap, but I kept my mind on the cards.

Even if I lost tonight, Samuel would never have me. It was as simple as that.

My hand wasn't the best at the table, I was sure of that. But my daddy had taught me well, and maybe being a woman made it easier for me to read the men sitting around me—or made it easier for me to keep them from reading me. A woman's best weapon is her ability to keep a secret.

I lay down my cards, and took back my destiny.

* * *

Where Margaret had gotten the money to secure a room at the hotel, I'll never know. I didn't care. Giddy on success and relief, I could only follow her.

The men who watched us go were jealous, and they had every reason to be.

She snuck a flask of whiskey up to our room, and we drank it and giggled like schoolgirls. Still, though, my hands shook as I held the deed.

"I should go home," I said. "He'll want to know what transpired."

Margaret rested a cool, long-fingered hand over mine, and I knew she understood. But I went on.

"Likely as not, though, he'll have drowned his worries in that last bottle he thinks I haven't found." I turned to Margaret, sitting on the bed beside me, and took her face in my hands. "We can be back tomorrow before he wakes up, and still have tonight."

Finally, I could kiss her again, in just the way I wanted to. Not rushed, not pretending, just the two of us, and all the time in the world.

I'd been needing her so badly and for so long that the touch of her soft lips to mine was nearly enough to send me flying. Neither of us wanted tender or slow. A moment later our teeth knocked together in our shared eagerness to kiss harder, closer, *now*.

Margaret was always beautiful to me, whether in her oldest dress, sweat beading her brow as she pounded the laundry; wearing trousers to join me when I rode out to inspect the back forty; or naked and rumpled in my bed. Now, though, I have to admit a certain baseness in that I found her astonishingly alluring in the short skirt and all-but-baring corset.

I couldn't help but snake my hand beneath the ruffles, gasping with delight when I found I'd been right that her nipple truly hadn't been restrained by the corset. Instead, it had hovered, barely covered by fabric, so close to my face all night long.

Then it was her turn to gasp—and my turn to thrill all the way down through my belly—as I rolled that tender nubbin between my fingers.

No more waiting. I pulled the fabric down, exposing the curves of her breasts above the tight line of the corset, and feasted on her rosy peaks, suckling and nipping until I swear the boning in her corset was the only thing keeping her upright.

That is, until I nudged her to lie back on the bed.

I worked my way beneath her skirts with the tenacity and skill of a prospector, and what I found was worth far more than gold to me.

She was sleek and open to me, tasting of honey and rainwater and promises. My only regret was that I couldn't see her face as I kissed her most intimate parts and slipped two fingers inside her. I could imagine, though. And I could hear her cry out as she spasmed around me, my sweet Margaret.

It was easy enough to get my shirt off, and she had me spinning in circles to release me from the wrapped cloth that bound my breasts. Men's clothes being as simple as they were, we had the luxury of undressing me completely before she paused, just for a moment, to stare at me with all the desire and love a woman could.

I'd so missed the feel of her mouth on me, kissing me everywhere, kisses and licks and nips until my body was on fire for her. Her own need sated for now, she felt she had more time to linger, and she laughed when I told her plainly that she would drive me mad before she was done.

With no corset to hold me, I was boneless and quivering by

the time she pressed a kiss against my hipbone, then brushed her hair against that same spot as she kissed me lower still.

Then there was nothing else in the world but Margaret and me.

My daddy had taught me to trust the cards and trust myself, not anything or anyone else. Still, when I'd bluffed my way through and laid down my winning hand that night, I'd felt a certain sense of destiny: two pair, queens up.

FUCKING WITH THE FARRIER

Rakelle Valencia

Every time I worked at her barn she stared at my ass. Now, I understand when a person is holding a horse with a farrier hanging onto a hoof beneath, bent over and butt end to them, that they're going to look. Who wouldn't? And how can it be avoided? It does make conversation difficult when most need to talk to my backside. Folks get over it, though, because it's just a normal event that happens when the horseshoer is working.

But I'm saying that this girl spent the entire time ogling my ass—no conversation. It got to the point that I could almost feel her caressing my buttocks, not to mention the age-old saying about being undressed by her eyes.

Yes, I liked it. I'm not bashful. And my hind end has always been one of my better assets, especially tied into a farrier's apron, like wearing a set of chinks, or short chaps. The ensemble tends to accentuate.

Okay, I knew she wanted me. But what was taking her so long?

Maybe the barn princess couldn't get her manicured finger-nails dirty with the hired help.

Or maybe I was just reading it all wrong. After all, my gaydar has been faulty from lack of use since I did my stint at Okla-homa Shoeing School. That was when I decided that women were women; lesbian, straight, or bi. It doesn't matter to me as long as they're willing to play. Hell, I just want to fuck them, not marry them.

She'd be a nice piece to fuck, too, I thought—all up in her own shit, but quiet-like. That's the kind I truly want to make scream.

I was working on the last horse's hooves, and she was still staring. There'd been no talk, just her big, round, blue eyes watching my taut asscheeks lined out in slim-fit Wranglers and framed by my leather apron with leg ties. I'd almost call that a boring morning, except for the fact that the horse was real interesting after having been foundered and needing degree pads to get it to walk visually sound. And the fact that there were several silent hours to daydream about what I'd like to do to her highness.

I placed the left hind leg on the barn's cement isle, scooped stand and tools out from the gelding's way, and asked her to walk him off. The gelding appeared to go sound, though I had adjusted his pads from four degrees to a three-degree on the left and a two-degree on the right to get him more comfortable and normal after eight weeks of good growth. He'd always have the rotation of bone, but his hoof could probably be shaped over time to hold the angles he needed without pads, though I didn't believe this horse would ever go barefoot again.

She had a good eye, for more than my ass, because she recog-nized that the Quarter Horse walked off with no gimping and put him back in his stall.

The place was ritzy. It catered to a lot of boarders, having trainers and giving lessons and hosting shows in their big indoor arena. The barn end had its own bathroom, tack room, viewing room to the attached indoor arena, and a well-appointed, locked office.

I used the horse-washing stall to soak my sweaty head under cool water from a hose. I doused my back where the sweat had stained my T-shirt before standing to shake like a dog and sip from the stream pouring forth. It was the same old ritual at this place, but today I felt like changing the ending.

Tools, hoof stand, anvil, and apron loaded back into the truck, I decided to meet her at the office door for my check instead of waiting by the truck. My short-cropped hair was spiky with wetness, and my streaked face was washed clean and already dried in the summer heat. I leaned against the open doorway, feeling the coolness of an air conditioner escaping past me.

She walked toward me, holding the check folded lengthwise like a prong between us. I stepped in to grasp the slip of paper while shoving the heavy door closed behind me. Enfolding her hand into my own, I directed it to my back pocket. "Is this where you want it?"

The act brought her a breath away from me, face to face. Her blue eyes watched mine intently, with no question and no answer. She didn't hesitate to shove that check into my back pocket, with a squeeze of my tight ass on the way out. Her other hand reached up to scrub through my damp spiky hair until she grasped what little there is at the back of my neck and tugged as her lips moved in to meet my own briefly.

Rumpling the bottom of my T-shirt, the woman jerked it up and over to rest securely around my shoulders behind my neck. My small, rounded breasts hadn't warranted a bra in this heat, so as the air conditioner blasted past my sweaty chest, bright red nipples swelled and hardened to points.

Our fingers entwined until she had control of my hands, thrusting them behind the small of my back as she leaned in to lick each nipple like a snake testing the air. Her tongue was momentarily warm on my flesh before it was gone and the room's frigid air raised goose bumps on my breasts.

The girl was a vamp, a vixen. She had been awaiting this opportunity and took no time in her pursuit. Her full mouth set upon first my left breast then my right, sucking, ending in kisses before trickling her lips along the length of my neck to my chin and claiming my mouth once again.

A hair tie acted as handcuffs as she took my wrists from being trapped low to hug the back of my head, slipping the band on one wrist and then wriggling my other wrist into it. Her tongue trailed a path through the middle of my chest to the piercing of my belly button, where it circled several times before diving in and out, pressing to the bottom of that tiny hole in a miniature fuckfest.

If my nipples aren't attached to my clit, like I've experienced with other women, my navel certainly is. The ministrations had my pelvis rocking while the crotch of my jeans was beginning to get soaked. Shit, I probably could have come if she hadn't stopped.

Cool hands swept along my heated ribs and waist, making me shiver. They clawed at the brass belt buckle. The rivet was easily popped open, and the gritty zipper sounded a protest as it was yanked apart from the sides.

She was on her knees by now. Her hot, wet tongue found the top of my shaved slit, moisture slicking the dryness in that first instant of ecstasy. Wranglers were shoved roughly to mid-thigh as she tested and teased my own growing slippery wetness with both tongue and fingers.

I threw my head back, shoving my cunt to her face. She lapped and licked and bit and tormented every inch of reddened, swollen flesh until I felt my knees would give way. At that instant, two fingers opened my twat and drummed on the G-spot. Then she turned me slightly as her mouth moved across the flat side of one butt cheek to the rounded mounds behind. Just as her thumb encircled my clit, her tongue assaulted my puckered rear hole, surprising me with a rim job the likes of which I've never experienced.

Trying to respond to each of the erotic sensations twisting and tantalizing the core of my body, I didn't know whether to thrust forward or squat backward, and instead, quivered in place as the most intense orgasm built inside of me.

Her thumb clamped harder in its circling of my clitoris. Her fingers inside grew more insistent upon my G-spot. And her tongue prodding the opening to my anus sent me over the edge.

I screamed like a little girl and writhed like the dying while pulling my own hair, and succumbing to the one I'd thought I would conquer that day.

I was doubled over and panting as she withdrew toward a knock resounding on the door. Bright light from the barn fell across a thick mahogany desk and an overstuffed, dark leather couch. I jerked in a leftover spasm and then reached to pull my clothes on properly.

She looked back at me once before escaping through that cracked doorway. After a few minutes, I staggered back to my truck.

In all my years of shoeing horses and fucking women, none of them had ever managed to kick the breath out of me. Until now.

MAN ENOUGH

Cecilia Tan

Beulah Kitt wasn't her real name, but it was who she was. Her legs were as long as her beguiling smile was wide, and with both of them wide, and more than a little guile, she had risen to the top of her profession. A night with Beulah Kitt at the famed Galloway Hotel was one of the prized treasures of the men of the West.

Few knew that she actually owned the Galloway and ran it behind the scenes. Most thought that Harley Lehman ran the place, and they assumed when he talked about the "owner" that the owner was some Gold Rush millionaire who'd settled in some far-off place like San Francisco.

Beulah opened the letter from Buffalo Jones herself when it came in with the stage. She was pleased to note that it appeared unopened. It seemed Jones had a cowhand who was ready to become a man. They were building the fella up something fierce on the trail, fixing to come into town in about a month's time.

Beulah Kitt smiled. They would all pitch in to buy the kid a night with her, and no one but her would do. It wouldn't be the first green, nervous virgin on Jones's crew Beulah had deflowered, either. A month? The poor boy. Imagine the performance anxiety.

Vance "Bulldog" Pattison hunched further down as the fire began to burn low and the inevitable talk about their next trip into Dawson began. Bulldog had hoped maybe once, just once, they'd give it a rest, but no, apparently the hands had a never-ending appetite for speculation and fantasizing about Miss Kitt's charms and the way she would ply them on poor, innocent Vance.

Vance's stomach churned. The talk had grown more and more graphic in recent days as the event became more imminent, though some of it made Vance laugh silently—there was no way some of these roughnecks had ever seen a woman's private parts, much less done half the things they described, except maybe for the one or two to whom Buff had given the Beulah treatment before. Vance ought to know, after all, how a woman's parts worked, because she was one.

Vance couldn't excuse herself from the ribbing and teasing, not if she was going to "be a man" about it. Well, another week and it'd be over, one way or the other. Either she'd have her night with Miss Beulah, get through it unexposed, or somehow swear the whore to silence. Or she'd be exposed at last.

"You better take care of business before you go see her," Skinny Jim said. "So's you don't shoot off the moment she tetches you and embarrass yourself."

Vance adjusted the package in her jeans. "You kiddin'? I been shootin' off every night just thinkin' about it. Since Buff done told me, I've had a nonstop boner."

That brought laughter from all around the campfire, some of it knowing—and after all, every word of it was true. Vance had been wearing a leather piece for the past three months, to make it look good. While working on saddles she'd made it out of glove leather. She even had a harder, stiffer one, which might have done to fool some virgin farm girl on her wedding night, with the lanterns out and the sky dark...

But it sure as hell wasn't going to fool Miss Beulah Kitt.

What had Buff been thinking, setting her up like this? Vance had thought for a while that maybe Jones even suspected she was a woman, but he'd seemed willing to look the other way, and he still did. Well, it would be what it would be. Vance excused herself to her bedroll, claiming tiredness but hefting her nonexistent balls meaningfully. More laughter, but no one seemed to mind. Some of them were probably off to do the same thing. Or...almost the same.

Vance settled in the dark and slipped her hand around the leather phallus, imagining that a gorgeous, long-legged woman like Beulah Kitt was wrapping slim fingers around her hot, stiff cock. She had the thing strapped on so if she tugged on it just right, one of the support straps pressed and pulled on her clit. If anyone ever did catch a glimpse of her wanking on a moonlit night, her hand moving under the blanket, it'd look exactly like they'd expect.

The added bonus was since she'd started doing it this way, she came harder than she'd come in her life. She didn't know if that was the cock, or the added fantasy of Miss Beulah Kitt.

She'd have to ask Buffalo Jones what color Miss Kitt's hair was.

Beulah looked up from her accounts. She could hear the sound of boots against the floorboards downstairs, voices starting to get raised as the afternoon crowd began to thicken. By sundown the place would be packed, but it was getting to be time to get dressed and make herself presentable.

She had no maid. She did her own hair, her own makeup, and even put her corset on herself, the laces already done in the back, while up the front there were tiny hooks and stays. She could tighten it further if she needed a little more shape, but a "loose" woman hardly needed the strict, breath-stealing constriction of a true lady's corset. She had learned early on in her career to put her boots on first, as once the thing was on, there was no bending over.

She flounced her skirts, making sure they were moving right as she walked back and forth in front of the mirror. It was important to show off her legs. It drew the eyes of the lustful away from her face, which was actually quite plain, her jaw too square, her lips too thin. Makeup did wonders, softening the lines, and she had always had thick eyelashes. She batted them in the mirror and pronounced herself ready for the evening.

Downstairs, Buffalo Jones was sitting at the bar, laughing with Frenchy about something, already halfway through a glass of whiskey. The hands were all sitting together around a table at the bottom of the stairs, and she nodded to them as she passed by on her way to Buff. The pale one in the corner, the one who looked like he didn't shave yet, that had to be the one.

She ran her hands across the yoke of Buff's shirt, and then settled her body next to him with one arm around his shoulders, just a half inch of her ass on his stool. "I got your letter, Buff," she purred into his ear. "You sure you ain't in town to see me yourself?"

Buff chuckled. "You know you're something special, darling. But no, not this time anyhow. You want to meet Vance, also known as 'The Bulldog'?"

Beulah laughed and clucked her tongue. "It's early yet, Buff. Let's let 'im stew for a while. Anticipation is part of the experience."

"Yeah, yeah. And the more my hands sit around here, the more they'll spend on food and drink."

"All part of the price, my dear." Beulah flashed Buffalo Jones a smile, then slipped away to greet another customer, her hand trailing off Buff's shoulder as she went, as if she didn't want to lose contact until the very last moment.

Vance climbed the stairs following Beulah Kitt like a lost miner following a rescuer with a lamp. The other hands had bought one or two rounds too many, she thought, and she clutched the banister like it was the railing on a rocking ship. Beulah's lacy, ruffly, bustle of an ass was swaying almost right in front of her eyes as she went up and up and up.

Vance wanted to reach up and grab it, but she was sure that any cowhand who did that would earn a smack and maybe even a boot out the door. The cheers and jeers of the other hands were still audible behind her, so she just concentrated on not falling down.

Was it the alcohol that made Vance's face burn such bright red that she could feel the heat coming off it? Or was it how Beulah had come up to their table, standing right behind Vance's chair, and run her hands down Vance's cheeks and said, "Sweet honey dear, have no fear, you'll be shaving in no time. Because tonight I will make you into a man."

Vance's heart pounded. What Beulah said had a kind of truth to it, too. If Vance could come out of this somehow unexposed, the night with Beulah would buy her a surefire image as a man. That would probably be good for two years if she stuck with Jones's crew, before she'd have to move on and start over again somewhere new, lying about her age as well as her sex. As it was, Buff's boys thought she was still in her teens. She was closer to twenty-five, and the harsh wind and sun were going to start showing on her face soon.

Still, it was a horse she'd ride as far as it could carry her.

Miss Beulah pulled open the doorway to a satin-bedecked boudoir and Vance followed her in. The moment the door shut behind them, Vance couldn't help herself. She wrapped her arms around Beulah from behind, the rigid ribs of the corset like a saddle in her arms, and breathed in the scent of the skin on the back of her neck. "You smell so pretty."

Beulah turned quicker than Vance would have thought possible and slapped her across the face. "None of that, mister. If you're going to spend a night with Miss Beulah, you do as Miss Beulah says."

"Yes, ma'am," Vance said, chagrined and wringing her hands. She'd left her hat downstairs. "I'm sorry, ma'am. I just got carried away."

"You don't touch and you don't look unless you're invited. Are we clear on that?"

"Clear as crystal, ma'am." Oh, God, Vance thought. There was no way she was going to get through this then. She'd been hoping the whore would let her take the initiative, and please her and satisfy her (hopefully) with such enthusiasm that...that maybe she wouldn't notice certain deficiencies? All right, it had been a stupid hope, but it had been a hope nonetheless. "I'm sorry. I'm...I'm normally real shy."

"You must be," Beulah said, looking Vance up and down. "Or Buff wouldn't have bothered to bring you to me." Her demeanor softened, and she looked both kind and alluring as she stepped close again and put her hands on Vance's belt buckle. "Come on, now, let me..."

"Er..." Vance blushed hard and jerked back, not quite ready for it all to come down around her. "I'm...I told you I was shy."

She swallowed as Beulah's hand slid down over the bulge in her jeans. "Funny," she said in a voice that was warm and breathy with desire. "You don't feel shy."

"I...well..." But then Vance moaned as Beulah ran her hand up and down her phallus, sending jolts of pleasure through her hidden clit. Vance thrust her hips, moving the strap back and forth against her clit and moaned again.

"Good boy," Beulah said. "Maybe you should come for me right now."

"Keep doing that, I will," Vance said, and it was nothing but true. "Let...let me lie down and I'll..."

Beulah pushed him back and Vance fell onto the bed. When had they moved so close to it? The whiskey here was strong. Beulah's hand went up and down, pressing hard and making everything in Vance's body tighten. She had her boots on the bed, but she didn't care, bucking up against that hand trying to get more stimulation. "Faster!" she begged.

"Hush, honey, I gotcha," Beulah crooned, tugging at it a bit through the thick denim.

Vance cried out as she came, thinking for half a second that God, wanking was never going to be the same again, and then not able to think anything else as the orgasm wiped out everything.

When thoughts flowed again, the first to emerge was: *Beulah Kitt made me cream in my pants*. The second was: *Here she comes*.

Beulah climbed astride the flushed, staring cowboy, her flouncing skirts coming to rest all around his groin. She settled her crotch against the seam, centered on the bulge, and made friction by sliding her hips forth and back. "Mm, how's this, boy? Reach up and grasp my waist."

Strong hands settled at the curve of her corset and helped her rock back and forth. God, how she loved to feel a firm grip like that. "That's it, yes..." She let Vance work her up and down his cock, falling silent as her breaths became more rapid and then small cries came forth in time with the motion. Oh, yes, that was the way, that was... She pressed her hands against his chest, her hips thrusting hard, again and again, and then clung to him, thrusting until she came. The orgasm went right through her, all through her, and she fell back because the corset would not let her fall forward.

At last she took a deep breath, wiped her brow with her forearm, and declared, "And you'll tell 'em you made Beulah Kitt come before you even took your trousers off."

The answer was a breathy, "Yes, ma'am."

Beulah righted herself, her skirts covering the sight of their crotches. She rose up onto her knees but didn't take her eyes from the cowboy's face. "Reach down there, boy, and take that pecker out. There's nothing I love more after coming hard like that than a good fucking."

Miss Beulah was good at poker, and she saw the tell, as Vance blanched a second when any other red-blooded American cowboy would have said "yee haw!" But then Beulah knew what to look for. "Go on," she said, quiet-like, and Vance's hands sped through belt buckle and all. Beulah reached between her legs to find her hand wrapped around a sizable but not ridiculous protuberance. She stroked it and found it reasonably smooth and stiff, but it could still use a little help.

"Reach into that drawer there, wouldya fella, and get that little jar out?"

Vance could reach the side drawer enough to pull it open but couldn't quite see into it or reach anything. Beulah leaned over and grabbed the grease. "Here you go. Butter up that corn cob of yours."

"Yes, ma'am." Vance was the perfect picture of lust, skin flushed and damp, hair flung back, and helpless with need.

Beulah wondered how many orgasms it would take to satisfy this one.

She took a bit of the grease and reached behind herself. "Gonna ride you, cowboy," she whispered.

Holy mother of Jesus Christ Almighty, Vance thought, as Beulah Kitt lowered herself onto her prick. *Holy shit, I'm fucking her.*

The motion was slow and smooth, until Beulah came to the bottom of the pole and rested there. "A nice fit," she said, and Vance almost wanted to ask, *Just blurt it out, you know it's not real, right? That's why you had me grease it up?*

But then Beulah was moving, and each time she lifted up and impaled herself again, another spark went through Vance. It was beyond arousing, it was overwhelming. Meanwhile Vance forgot all about the not touching without being told, and ran her fingertips along the top of Beulah's corset, where the creamy flesh of her bosom was softest. Beulah seemed to have forgotten about it, too, though, because she didn't scold, just sighed and rocked harder.

Time stopped moving for Vance. There was fucking Beulah, and then still fucking Beulah. This time release was gradual in coming, but Vance could already tell it was going to be even bigger than the previous one, which had up until then been the hardest she'd ever come in her life.

"Oh, God, Miss Beulah..." Vance couldn't quite bring herself to say the rest of it, which was "fuck me until I come," but maybe it was evident enough. Beulah rode her cock like a mad Cherokee, beginning to whoop. Vance wondered if they could hear it downstairs; they probably could. That was her last thought about anything for a while outside of Beulah and heat and friction and oh, God just one more and I'm going to explode.

When Beulah's head finally touched the pillow next to

Vance's, she was out of breath (damn corset) and thirsty but too tuckered out to pour herself a glass of water from the pitcher on the stand. Beulah closed her eyes briefly and felt a light touch on her forehead, her temple. Vance was brushing the hair out of her eyes.

She cleared her throat but didn't open her eyes. "That was a mighty fine ride, bronco. But don't get any romantic ideas about how horses love their riders and vice versa."

The hand withdrew and the answer came back in a rough half-whisper. "Yes, ma'am."

"Gonna tell you a bedtime story now, cowboy," Beulah said softly, holding back a yawn. "There was a young one I deflowered once, back when I was just the top attraction here, and before I...and Harley bought this place." Jesus, she had to be careful, but post-orgasmic bliss made her sloppy. "There was a young cowhand who was working for a boss named Black Bill. Black Bill, as you might've guessed, wasn't black-skinned but black-hearted, and he mistreated his hands pretty bad. He was boss of a big herd, though, and working for him paid well, even if they said he was a sodomite and a sinner of the worst kind."

Beulah opened her eyes to make sure Vance was still listening and hadn't drifted off to sleep. "Anyway, this hand of his came into town one day with the lot of them, and caused a ruckus of a sort, saying that he wouldn't leave town again until he'd had a night with me. Now the money he had from Bill so far wouldn't buy a night with me, and he and Bill had a bust-up first thing when Bill wouldn't give him more. That got the town all abuzz, of course. So then when he got out of the hoosegow for fighting and disturbing the peace, he started challenging all the card sharks in town to poker, trying to increase his stake enough to buy that dream night with me.

"He was so determined that of course it was the talk of the

town, and in the end, when he came up just shy of the amount needed, Harley Lehman himself spotted him the difference. That hand was the proverbial cock of the walk for the longest time after that, and never did go back with Bill and his crew when they left town, but hooked on as a boss himself with Jim Masters."

She watched as Vance's eyes widened at the mention of a familiar name. "You're talking about Buff, aintcha."

She nodded. "A night with me was the best thing that ever happened to Jones. I didn't know it at the time, but apparently before that not only Bill but the other hands on that crew thought maybe Buff wasn't...man enough."

"You mean...?"

"He liked to take it up the ass," Beulah said, delighting in the blush that crept over Vance's cheeks at such crude language. She laughed. "And once a cowboy gets that kind of reputation, well, you know, he might find himself..."

"The butt of jokes?" Vance tried.

"That is one way of putting it," Beulah agreed. "Anyway, Buffalo Jones knows as well as anybody that a night with me is a good way to solidify one's masculine image." She trailed her hand up Vance's now slimy thigh but stopped short of touching the strap that she knew ran between Vance's legs.

"And you're...you're okay with it?"

Beulah smiled. Such a naïve thing. "Let's just say that my good friend Harley is a good friend of Buff's, too. You stick with Buff."

Vance listened to the story with growing wonder, and in the end all she could really say was, "Thank you. Thank you for your help, and your hospitality, ma'am."

"Anytime, cowboy, anytime," Miss Beulah said. "Now if you really want to give 'em something to talk about, we ought to make a reappearance downstairs. I'll be properly bowlegged, you blush or boast or both, and then we oughtta come back up here. You'll be stiff as new leather by then again anyway, right?"

"Right." Vance's head was still spinning a little with all that Beulah had said, and not said. She'd never come out and said "I know you're a woman," had never even acknowledged that Vance didn't have a real dick.

Maybe it didn't matter. It wasn't until two days later, when Buff and Vance were riding together on the edge of town, that Vance finally said thank you, a real thank-you, to his boss. As well as, "She said stick with you, so I figure I better."

Buff laughed. "She's a regular font of wisdom, ain't she? Well, you know what they say, you can't fake a faker."

Vance blinked. "What? You don't mean she's a man?"

"Beulah? Naw. But she can't hold that place down by herself. Too many wolves circling around who think a woman can't do it on her own. So she becomes Harley when she needs to do serious business. Don't you be telling nobody that, of course."

"Of course." Vance took what she was told at face value and didn't think any more of it. But later, lying alone under the stars, she got to thinking. She had no proof either way that Beulah was a woman or a man. She could have easily been a man in woman's clothes. Vance never touched her between the legs or saw her breasts. Or it could be as Buff thought, that she was a woman but played the part of a man when she needed to.

Maybe it really doesn't matter, Vance thought. *She's man enough.*

THE HIRED HAND

Delilah Devlin

The air didn't move inside the dimly lit barn. It was hot, musty, redolent of fresh hay and horses—and with ripe, sensual anticipation. Work was done for the day. Decision time had finally arrived.

A lariat landed around my shoulders, and I pressed my lips together to hide a smile. I struggled against the waxed poly-nylon, but the rope cinched tighter. Then hands dragged it downward, scraping past nipples already spiking hard against thin cotton.

A hot breath gusted against my ear. "Anything a man can do I can do better," came a whispering rasp.

"Why do I feel like breaking into song?" I muttered. I jerked against the rope, but my arms were pinned to my sides. It was only a show of resistance. We both knew I was hot for what came next. "Should have been a little more specific when I placed that damn ad," I said, legs braced apart to keep from tumbling to the fresh hay spread on the floor of the stall.

A blanket landed on the ground in front of me.

Muffled footsteps drew near again. "Should have said, 'Only a cowboy with a dick need apply.' "

I tossed back my hair and aimed a glare over my shoulder. Then my glance fell to what the cowboy in question held in her slender hand. "Looks like you still would've qualified."

Ari lifted both eyebrows, a grin wreathing her face. She wagged the dildo in front of me, taunting me. "Tell me you're not sorry it was me who showed up."

My breath caught. Even in the fading light inside the barn, my hired hand's eyes glittered brightly. "I still have reservations that you can get the job done," I lied. "I might have been seeking someone to wrangle some horses, but I'd hoped for a little action on the side, too."

"Like I said, whatever a man can do..." A strong arm wrapped around my waist. "Want me to prove it?"

"Oh, God," I moaned as the dildo trailed down the side of my cheek. "Fuck me, Ari. Fuck me with your big cock."

A snicker sounded a moment before teeth bit into my earlobe. Then her arms dropped away, and cool air rushed against my back. "Gonna be good if I untie you?"

"I don't make promises I can't keep," I ground out.

"You always make me work damn hard," she growled.

"I warned you I'm not an easy boss."

Ari stepped in front of me, dark eyes narrowed, skimming over my frame. She drew a knife from the sheath strapped to her leather belt and lifted one brow. "Sure you want to lose this shirt?"

"I'm not going to help you. I told you I'm not into girls."

"And I love making you eat your words." The dull side of the knife glided between my breasts. I shivered as cool steel pressed in a narrow path downward. Ribbed cotton parted, exposing the white skin beneath the ring of tan that ended at my neck.

As the lacy center of my bra was laid bare, one corner of Ari's lips quirked upward. "Don't know why you even bother. I like watchin' 'em bounce." The bra met the same fate as the shirt, popping open as soon as the lace was severed.

My breasts quivered, rising with my sharp gasp. The cool air inside the barn wafted around my nipples. My relief as the knife disappeared and my breasts sprang free had me sighing before I remembered I should be putting up more of a front. "That's coming out of your wages."

Ari's fingers plucked my nipples. "Worth every penny, too." Then she ducked, and warm, wet lips enclosed one ripening bud.

My head fell back, and my eyes slid closed as she suckled softly. God, had it only been two days?

I set aside the shovel at the sound of a horn honking in the distance. Heaving a deep sigh at the interruption, I tugged off my work gloves, lay them over the top of the stall I'd been mucking out, and headed toward the open doors. Sunshine beat down on my head as I stepped outside. I lifted a hand to shield my eyes from the bright glare.

A white pickup sat in front of the house, a shadowy figure at the wheel. The cab door groaned as it swung outward. The driver slid to the ground. Slim calves encased in wash-softened blue jeans ended above a polished set of cowboy boots.

Maybe someone had come about the ad I'd placed for help. Maybe someone strong, not afraid of a little hard work, and in need of a paycheck. I'd posted the "Help Wanted" notice in the local paper over a week ago and had begun to regret the fact I'd stated the wage. It wasn't much. Most of the men who'd applied were too old or too inexperienced. I was getting desperate for a little relief.

And if the next cowboy happened to be reasonably attractive...

Well, I hoped they might overlook my sun-baked skin and the crow's feet that had grown a little deeper with the passing of another summer. Maybe they'd like a little added "bonus" with their paycheck along with room and board. I'd been through a long drought of bed partners and wasn't going to be too fussy.

The figure that appeared with the slam of the door made my shoulders dip in disappointment. I needed a man. A strong set of shoulders and a sturdy back. The slender woman walking toward me didn't appear to have the muscle to work the horses and help with the outside chores. And she was too damn pretty for my peace of mind.

I drew a deep breath, preparing to be polite but trying to come up with an excuse for turning the woman away that wouldn't sound like I'd made up my mind as soon as I'd noted the high set of her breasts and the curve of her narrow hips.

"You Miss Lacey Kudrow?" the woman asked, her voice sounding a little breathless. Her dark gaze flicked over me briefly before returning to lock with mine.

A jolt of unwanted attraction flared deep inside me, but I nodded. "What can I do for you?"

A casual shrug warred with the tension in her shoulders. "I've come about the job."

"You do know I'm looking for a wrangler," I said, my doubt flavoring my response. "Someone who knows *his* way around a horse. The job calls for a trainer, maintenance of the pens, mucking out stalls, currying—"

"You think I don't know how to do all that?" She lifted her cowboy hat and shook out her hair, which fell thick and straight to her shoulders.

The sun caught glints of copper in the dark brown strands,

and my breath hitched. Christ, it didn't matter if the girl could do the job or not. I couldn't let her stay. Horny as I was, I guessed I might be a lot less fussy than I'd ever dreamed.

The woman's face screwed up into a stubborn frown. "You're boarding horses…"

"And training them—for personal use mostly, but I also have a couple of reining horses."

"Plan to enter any competitions?"

I didn't like the dark glint entering her eyes or the way her lips began to curve. "Maybe…"

"Thought I recognized your name," she said, softer now. "You placed in the Breeder's Classic last year."

"Yeah, with Painted Lady." Because I was beginning to feel guilty about how rude I'd been, I relented a bit. "You into the sport as well?"

Her head shook. "It's not what I do, but I like to catch any horse events in the area. I barrel-race. But I lost my horse." Her nose wrinkled. "Lost my boyfriend, too, but I don't miss him near as much. Needed to leave the rodeo circuit for a while, and here I am."

I sighed. "Look, I'm sure you know a lot about horses, but what I really need is someone to help me with the day-to-day. You look…nice, but…"

"You think I'll cry over a broken nail? That I can't rasp a hoof or lift a bale of hay?"

"I'm just saying," I said slowly, wishing I hadn't decided to be polite. "I don't think you'll be happy here."

"How about a trial? Give me a couple of days," the woman said, her lush lips settling into a straight line. "See how it works, then make up your mind whether you want me."

A wash of heat flooded my cheeks. *Whether you want me…*

"My name's Ariana Estevez," she said and held out her hand.

I wished my nails were trimmed and my palms not so rough, but the hand that slid across mine had its own share of calluses.

She wrapped her fingers around my hand and pumped. "Two days," she said.

Because I was exasperated with my lack of backbone, I turned around without answering and ambled into the barn, more worried about betraying my interest than being thought rude.

"I guess I'll unpack later," Ariana said, striding past me and laying claim to the shovel. She slipped off her pressed chambray shirt and hung it on a post. Then, dressed only in a thin tank that hugged nicely rounded breasts, she dug into a pile of ripe manure.

That first day, I had no complaints about her work. Ariana dug into a long list of chores, keeping up a steady rate of conversation that passed the hours as we groomed horses, readying them for the weekend when the owners would show up to take them out on the trails. As long as we stayed busy I managed to tamp down my unfortunate attraction. But work ended just before dark, and now I didn't know how to avoid her without retreating to my bedroom.

Footsteps scuffed across the planked porch, and Ariana lowered herself beside me on the bench overlooking the paddock. From the corner of my eye, I noted the damp hair and the bare expanse of skin that shone like warm honey beneath a pair of cutoff shorts. She'd bathed and smelled faintly of flowers.

I intended only a quick glance at my companion, but my gaze landed on another thin tank top, this one buttoned down the front with the upper two opened. The shadowy wedge of skin between her breasts was bare. Nipples, unfettered by any bra, sprang against the pink cotton.

"Thought since it was just us girls…" she drawled.

With heat flooding my cheeks, I turned away, unable to meet Ariana's lopsided smile.

"Guess it can get a little lonely out here," she said softly.

"It can," I said, feeling a little breathless. "But I like the quiet."

"Seeing anyone?"

My head swung back.

Ariana's brow was arched. "Just wondering. Pretty woman like you living all alone out here…seems a waste."

"Like having a man underfoot to feed and please would make my life easier?" I'd tried that and failed miserably. The breakup had nearly broken me and devastated my bank account.

"Sorry, didn't realize I'd struck a nerve."

"Well, you did. How about we just drop it?"

"So, there's no one steady in your life…?" I shot her a hot glare, which had her lips pursing in a silent whistle. "Look, I know you're not comfortable around me. Want me to guess why? Or how about you just tell me instead of making me play 'twenty questions'?"

"Like you said," I murmured uncomfortably, blood starting to pound against my temples, "it gets a little lonely out here. For the most part, people only come to ride on the weekends."

She snorted. "Ever have a girl?"

Shock had me stiffening and wondering if I'd jumped to a wrong conclusion about where this was heading because my mind was already in a very nasty gutter. "Do you mean, working here?" I asked, knowing I sounded like I'd strangled on something. "No."

Her gaze narrowed. "I meant…ever have a girl…in your bed."

My breath caught. Was she taunting me? "No."

"Not once? Funny, I thought…" Ariana shook her head. "I didn't mean to offend."

We sat in silence for a few strained minutes. But I, who never felt easy in my own skin, never knew the right words to explore a possibility so ripe with dangerous undertones, cleared my throat. "What did you think?"

"That you liked what you saw."

My lips parted. And unexpectedly, moisture filled my eyes. "You must get all kinds of people coming on to you."

"All kinds, both sexes." Her lips curved. "But I don't mind *you* looking…" Her head fell back, and she shook out her wet hair. The action made her breasts shiver in a delightful way.

I bit my bottom lip and stared as Ariana's nipples spiked hard, elongating as I watched.

Her arm reached out slowly and draped across the back of the bench. Her fingers played with a lock of my hair. "You do it with all your hired hands?"

There was no use playing like I didn't understand her meaning. "Of course not."

"But it's nice, isn't it? The convenience of it?"

"It's only convenient if the cowboy understands rules."

Her finger slid along the outer curve of my ear. "Do you have special rules for a cowgirl?"

I closed my eyes briefly, and then aimed a glare her way, hoping she didn't see how unnerved I was becoming. "I've never had a female hand."

Ariana's hand slipped over my shoulder and reached down to palm my breast through my shirt. "Is it so different? A man's hand?"

"As night and day."

"Really? It's just a hand with fingers…" Her thumb and forefinger plucked at my nipple.

"Completely different," I said, clamping my lips against a tiny sigh. "I've never felt so..."

"Hot?"

"Uneasy," I blurted.

"That's not good. Want me to stop?" she said, giving my breast another tentative caress.

I opened my mouth to tell her yes, but instead found myself whispering, "I want you to take off your shirt."

Ariana's head jerked back and a startled laugh ripped the air. Her arm slipped from around my shoulder, and she turned sideways in the seat. "Anytime you want to stop, just let me know," she said softly. "I won't push. Tomorrow, it'll be like nothing ever happened. If that's what you want."

Because I felt a little winded by her enthusiasm, I shook my head. "Since I don't know what the hell I want, I guess I'll just play it by ear."

Ariana smiled, and then gripped the hem of her tank and pulled it over her head. Without meeting my gaze, she cupped her breasts, lifting them and massaging the slight curves. "I'd really like it if you did this for me. My breasts hurt after a long day smashed inside a sports bra."

Modesty seemed a little ridiculous at this point. I'd asked to see them, after all—it was only a small step to actually touch them. And the sight did make my palms itch. I reached for her breasts and cupped them gently. The nipples scraped deliciously. Her breasts were light and firm, her skin unbelievably soft. Especially the dark ovals of her areolas, which felt like velvet beneath the pads of my fingers.

Her gaze met mine, and she offered me a smile. Then she looked toward the road leading up to the house. "We're far enough off the road here that we could both get naked. Want to do that?"

"It's still light."

Her glance cut to mine. "Worried I won't like what I see?"

Absurdly, I knew I wouldn't be as modest if a man sat oppo-
site me. "I'm older. Not as firm. And I'm carrying too much
weight."

"Think I haven't already checked your ass out? I'm pretty
sure I'm going to like everything you show me. Besides, doesn't
this feel unbelievably naughty?"

I felt a smile tug at the corners of my lips. "Contrary to what
you must think about me, I don't hop into bed with a man this
quick."

"I'll take that as a compliment." Ariana stood and pushed
her shorts down her slender hips, standing unashamedly naked
in the dwindling light.

I shut my eyes, praying for courage, and rose from my seat. I
untucked my shirt from my jeans and slowly unbuttoned it. The
bra came next, and I shivered as my nipples grew stiff, dimpling
as soon as I let them out to play. My jeans and boots took a little
longer, because my hands were shaking, but by the time I was as
nude as Ariana, I was smiling, albeit tightly, too.

Ariana's hands grasped both my breasts, lifting them, forcing
the heavy mounds upward. She bent and stroked her tongue
over one peak, then the other. "Nice, Lacey. Very nice."

Then she circled behind me, her hands gliding over my
buttocks, around again, until she was gliding over my belly,
which had begun to quiver. "You know I'm going to want to
taste everything."

Moisture, quick and hot, slid between my folds. "Shall we go
inside?" I rasped.

"Afraid the coyotes might see?" she teased.

"I want something soft under my knees." I reached out
tentatively, and twined my fingers with Ariana's, then tugged

her through the door, leading her through the living room and down the darkened hallway to my bedroom. Inside, I didn't flinch when Ariana turned on the overhead light. She headed straight for the bed.

I hovered in the doorway, caught in a moment of indecision. *God, could I really do this?*

Ariana climbed onto the mattress and sighed as she stretched diagonally across the coverlet. "Mmm...it's so soft." Her legs fell open. Her sex, swollen and deep, dark pink, glistened. Her eyelids dipped blissfully as her hand stroked her darkly furred mound.

My mouth grew dry at the lush invitation. "Don't go to sleep on me," I quipped, trying to cover my awkwardness.

Her lips pursed in a mischievous grin. "As if! I'm waiting for that sweet pussy to slide right over my lips."

A cowboy had said the same thing to me, long ago. From him it had sounded crude, and I'd hesitated. From Ariana, with a naughty light glittering in her eyes, it was wicked without seeming tawdry.

"How about you let me show you how to love a woman?" she said softly.

I hadn't realized I was worried about not knowing exactly how to arouse this woman, and I relaxed, letting Ariana pull me down beside her until we faced each other on the bed.

"I travel a lot when I'm on the circuit," Ariana said, tucking a lock of my hair behind my ear. "And sometimes I have different partners, women and men, that I pick up. I don't care too much about whether I please them. I only worry about whether they'll please me." Her finger rimmed my lips slowly. "Lacey, I want to show you everything they taught me."

Ari had opened up a whole new world of sensual delights in

that first night. And I had been ravenous to discover more ever since. Not that I was ready to declare that girl-sex was my new preference.

I liked dick. Liked a powerful man stroking deep. Strong, muscled arms encircling me. But lovers, the stick-around kind, hadn't been in the cards for me.

I sighed as Ari's hands unlooped my belt, loosened my jeans and slid beneath the waistband to cup my generous ass.

We stood face-to-face in the stall, our gazes clashing. "Think I don't know what you like about guy-sex?" Ari stepped back and stripped, making quick work of her clothing until her jeans slid down her hips. She wore no panties, just a black harness that wrapped around her waist, more straps disappearing between her legs. She reached down to the blanket where she'd tossed the dildo and inserted it into the fitting at the front of the harness. The dildo, a long, sculpted gel with exaggerated veins and a pair of firm balls, bobbed between her legs.

"Jesus," I moaned, my pussy already anticipating the stretch and beginning to throb.

"Wait here," Ari said, her voice tightening.

"As if I have a choice?" I muttered.

Moments later, Ari reappeared, carrying a wooden sawhorse which she set in the hay and then draped with the blanket. She unlooped the end of the rope that she'd tied off on a post and began to wrap it in a coil, bringing me closer.

I kept up the pretense of reluctance, dragging my feet, but the cock was already working on me. My cunt was flushed with heat and growing moist. My breasts were so hard and tight I drew back my shoulders, inviting Ari's gaze, begging silently for her to lean down and bite the straining tips.

But Ari ignored the jut of my chest, gripped my shoulders, and shoved me face-first over the sawhorse.

"This will work better if you take off my clothes, too," I said hopefully.

A soft snort behind me told me Ari wasn't taking suggestions, but my pants were pushed past my buttocks, and the dildo nudged between them.

"Jesus," I whispered again, letting out a deep breath when the moistened tip glided down and slid along my slick folds. I tried to make more space for it, but my clothing kept my thighs bound tightly together. Hands clutched my hips, and the dildo glided slowly forward and back, and then withdrew.

One foot was lifted and my boot was removed.

"Guess I was right. It's easier without clothes," I mumbled.

The other came off and my jeans were jerked down my thighs. At last I was naked. I braced apart my legs, opening my sex, begging again for attention.

A rustling sounded behind me, and then moist kisses landed on my bottom. A tongue glided down the crevice between my asscheeks, circling slowly over my asshole, just long enough to make me worried, but then she stroked downward. Teeth gripped my outer labia, nibbling gently, and then lips sucked. Her wicked tongue stroked into my entrance, while a humming groan vibrated against me. Fingers circled over and over on my clit while lips tugged and tongue stroked. I rose on my toes to tilt my ass higher.

Blood rushed to my head and sex. My clit swelled painfully. Then hands smoothed the backs of my thighs as Ari rose behind me and reached over to grip my shoulders, raising my torso while the smooth gel cock prodded my opening.

"God, please...make it deep."

A slap jerked me, heat rising in short parallel ribs on my buttocks. The cock found my opening, dipped inside, and held still. "Think I don't know how to fuck?" Ari whispered. "I've had miles of dick inside me. I've fucked miles of cunt."

The words, so coarse, spoken in her tight choked voice, elicited a thrill that released a wash of liquid, engulfing the head of the cock poised at my entrance. "I wish you could feel what you do to me..."

"Think I can't? Think I'm not going to get off, too? You're wet and sucking at my cock. When I slam into you, I'm gonna feel it right against my clit."

"Jesus, just do it. God, Ari." I rose on toes again, trying to back onto the cock, but she followed the movement, and the crown slipped from my channel.

"Hold still. Don't help. Just feel." A hand gripped the back of my hair, lifting my head, arching my back, and then her hips slammed forward, and the thick cock rammed deep, pressing deep into my channel, gliding straight until the firm balls slapped my clitoris.

I bucked hard, not caring that she pulled my hair.

Ari wound her hand, tugging my head higher. Only that one hand held me suspended. My arms were still cinched at my sides and my abdomen was stretched, shuddering as she rocked forward and back, plowing deep, rutting like a man into my cunt until it felt hot, the soft tissues abraded by the heavy, veined ridges.

"I need more," I sobbed.

"What's that?" she said, halting her movements when her belly was pressed against my ass and her cock so deep I felt it at the mouth of my womb. "A cock isn't enough for you?"

"I need more."

"Gotta be a little more specific, *chica*. Want my tongue, my fingers? Will that be enough?"

"Yes. Your fingers on my clit. Your cock ramming deep."

Ari came out of me, and her hand let go of my hair. My body

sagged over the sawhorse. She drew me up gently, shoved the structure to the side, then helped me to lie down on the blanket she'd spread on the fragrant straw.

"I'm gonna fuck you like a man. Face-to-face. But you know why this is gonna be better than anything you've ever had?"

As her fingers entered me, I gasped and lifted my knees, letting them splay wide. I shook my head. "Why's it gonna be better?"

"Because I'm a girl. I know what your clit needs, know just how to touch it to make you spark like a wildfire."

She bent, lifted the hood cloaking my engorged clit, and suckled it, nursing it with her lips. When I began to moan, she drew back, a wicked light in her eyes again. "Not yet, baby." She came over me, her breasts pressing into mine, her tight little points rubbing my areolas.

My thighs widened and lifted to bracket her narrow hips. The dildo nudged my entrance and slid inside.

With my belly curved toward hers, the base of the cock slammed against my bared clit. It was enough. I was coming apart. But she lifted her belly and slid a hand between us. Her wet fingers circled on the rigid knot of nerves, and she resumed stroking inside me as she braced herself on one arm.

I met her gaze, read the warmth and approval in her expression. Saw the excitement rising in her darkening cheeks. Her eyes slid closed, her head fell back, and she jolted her hips against mine, losing rhythm as her own orgasm began to spiral.

I curled beneath her, latched onto a nipple, and bit the tip.

With her finger stroking my clit, her cock driving deep inside, and my mouth filled with soft heat, I exploded.

Our cries echoed against the wooden walls. Horses snorted; hooves shuffled uneasily. Then silence fell around us as we both eased to the ground.

She nuzzled my cheek, and her lips slid along my jaw and

then lifted. We kissed, lips softly smoothing like butter in shallow circles. The kiss was divine. Rapturous.

When my legs unwound from her waist, and she arched her back to come out of me, I gave a shaky laugh, hoping she hadn't heard the jagged edge of it. "Guess I'll have to give you a raise."

Her gaze narrowed. "Don't forget who's still tied up."

"The rope's beginning to itch."

"Poor baby," she said, her lips gliding along the rope, kissing the skin rubbed a fiery red. "Was I a little rough?"

"Ari…"

Her head came up, her gaze locking with mine.

"That's the best I've ever had. But there's a problem."

Her expression grew shuttered. "Say it. It's not like you've spared my feelings up to this point. I've been the one trying to prove up my claim."

"I need the rope gone, first," I said quietly.

She dragged me up and loosened the loop, slipping it over my head.

"The cock, too," I said, pointing my chin toward the gel cock still bobbing between her legs.

Her chest fell, and she kept her gaze down as she removed it.

I came to my knees and placed my hand in the center of her chest and shoved.

She fell backward with a gasp, half on the blanket, half on the prickly straw.

I straddled her waist and bent over her, my mouth an inch from hers. "I've let you do me, but I've never given you a damn thing."

"Not true," she said, her voice thickening.

"Shut up. I thought I wasn't committing to girl-sex if I never gave you pleasure. That's gonna change right now."

Her brown eyes blinked. Her lips curved upward at both corners. "Think you know how, little virgin?"

"I think you're gonna demand a whole lot more from me from now on."

"Mmm..." she moaned, her eyelids sliding downward. "I can think of a place or two I want those soft lips of yours to kiss. Sure you're up for it, Lace?"

"No, baby. I'm going *down*."

Then with my face diving between her legs, burrowing into her pussy, I couldn't pretend any longer that I'd hungered for the stroke of a tongue, the thrust of skilled fingers, and a hard cock from a man.

Ari's essence, richly and pungently feminine, spilled onto my greedy tongue, and I lapped it up like the starving woman I was.

Her fingers dug into my hair, holding me there as her hips rocked gently up and down. I applied all the lessons she'd taught me about how I liked to be touched to bring her pleasure.

I eased two fingers into her moist cunt and swirled my tongue over her clit. I latched my lips around the knot when it grew engorged and sucked hard, slipping another finger inside her and pumping relentlessly as her movements grew more desperate and her breaths jagged.

At last, I felt the tremors ripple inside her. She shoved her pussy into my face, her abdomen curling toward me, her fingers raking my scalp. Her cries were thin, warbling almost, and then she collapsed against the blanket, her legs splayed like a woman who'd been thoroughly loved.

I crawled upward, snuggled next to her spent body, and cupped her breast, massaging to soothe her now.

Her hand covered mine and squeezed. "I take it..." she gasped, "that you don't have any more reservations about whether I can do the job."

"You have any about me? Besides, one doesn't have a thing to do with the other," I said, pressing my lips to the nipple nearest my mouth.

"Ah, hell. Don't make me think."

"You're fine, cowgirl. You've got the job."

Her gaze met mine. "And this? Gonna let this hired hand have the pleasure of your company every night?"

I scraped my callused palm across her belly, and slid my fingers into her folds. "It's not so different. Your hand. Mine." I teased her sex with shallow grazes and then tucked them inside.

"Glad you figured that out," she said, growing breathless again.

"Not a man's hand," I admitted gruffly. "*Better.*"

NIGHTMARE

Jean Roberta

Sparkling snow stretched out in all directions beyond the fences that marked the boundaries of Julia's property. I used to feel sorry for my cousins because they were trapped on a boring farm like Julia's, but now I liked the isolation and tranquility. A pale sun shed its light on the house, the barn, and a stand of frost-covered trees. All this had been built and planted by Julia's grandparents.

I had known Julia ever since I first "came out" by ordering my first beer in the town's one gay bar. She had even hosted Christmas parties on her farm for the town's lesbian community, but something about her always seemed just beyond my reach. She didn't like gossip and only spoke when she had something to say. This was an art that some of us were still trying to learn.

"Want to earn your keep, girl?" Julia asked me on the night I arrived. I had driven for three hours, not really knowing where I was going, and showed up at her door with no warning.

I knew that was uncouth, but once I was there, I couldn't

just turn around and leave. I knew she wasn't running a guest ranch, so offering her money for my stay would have looked tacky. She'd let me in readily enough, though, and her question was fair.

"Sure," I told her. She gave me a steady look.

Holy fuck. Or unholy fuck. Did she know how I had survived when I couldn't find a straight job? I knew she called herself a feminist, but I didn't really know what she meant by that. Omigod, what did she think of me?

"You can help me with chores in the morning. There's plenty to do around here."

Her deep brown eyes looked unreadable until she smiled, crinkling up the laugh-lines at their corners. Her half-breed cheekbones caught the light from the fire in the stone fireplace. Her black hair, streaked with silver, hung in a long braid down her back, a rope of hair pulled off her face to stay out of her way. I noticed how Julia's breasts rose and fell with each breath under her loose cotton sweater.

I had heard the rumors about why Julia stayed out here alone instead of selling or renting out the farm. Looking at her, I could hardly believe she was as scary as rumor had it.

"I don't expect you to milk the cows," she said. "You might want to feed the goats. They like visitors, but they'll try to chew off your buttons. Don't let them."

Chewing buttons. I wanted to see Julia's generous breasts and taste her proud nipples. That wouldn't shock her. She had been an out dyke since she was a teenager, but I didn't know how stone she might be. I would be glad to offer her my nipples to suck, if that appealed to her. Maybe not a good idea. I had a dirty mind, and I was lucky she couldn't read it.

I felt the heat in my face and hoped she would think I was just responding to the warmth of the fire.

"You can feed Misty, the new pony, and groom her if you want, but she doesn't like to be ridden. I won't really start training her until spring."

I wanted to meet the little horse who didn't like to be ridden, a kind of stone pony. I could sympathize with an animal that didn't want to carry humans around on her back. Who would? I knew about ponyplay as part of a kinky human lifestyle, but were real horses ever kinky? I wondered how Julia could afford to keep an animal that was never likely to earn her feed.

On earlier visits I had seen Julia riding her full-sized gelding, Starblanket. She looked totally in control when she rode, as though nothing could be more natural. I couldn't imagine feeling that comfortable on a horse.

"You ever shovel shit?" She was grinning. "In town they all shoot the shit, but here we shovel it. If you want that job, you're welcome to it."

I didn't know what to say.

"I'll show you tomorrow. I bet you want some sleep now. You can stay in the guest room tonight." Her offer sent a jolt up my spine. *Just tonight? Until she invites me to warm her own bed, or form a threesome with her and Farmer John, or until she kicks my sorry ass out the door?* I was disappointed but relieved, anxious but hopeful.

She led the way up to the second floor. When we got there, I followed her into a clean, cozy room where a black cat was already sleeping on a patchwork quilt. I saw an old wooden bureau with an adjustable mirror attached, a bookcase full of old books, and chintz curtains.

For a moment, I felt as if Julia was debating whether to kiss me goodnight or pull me into the room and throw me down on the bed. As she lingered, my ever-hopeful clit woke up and let me know it wanted attention.

"I'll see you in the morning," she said. "I'm usually up with the roosters, but you can sleep in, since you're a guest. You can make yourself breakfast in the kitchen. There's eggs, bread, bacon, cereal, and fruit—help yourself. Sleep tight, Chris."

Did I really see a wicked smirk on her face as she turned away from me? I reminded myself that she was generous to let me stay in her house. I had no right to expect more than that.

I opened my backpack and spread out the few things I had brought with me. Then I looked in the mirror. The face that looked back was sickly-pale, dominated by dark eyes with dark shadows under them. My brown hair, gelled into shape that morning, now looked sodden. I had been admired for maintaining the same slim body since my teens, but now I just looked malnourished, like a street person of no fixed address. Or maybe I was just seeing the way I felt.

I couldn't stay here indefinitely. I would have to go back to town and resolve things. Sooner or later, I would have to face Bert—my ex-girlfriend now and for all time—and her friends. The lesbian community where I had spent my whole adult life was like a small, dusty town in a vintage Western: not big enough for the two of us.

I turned off the light, pulled off my clothes, and slid under the sheets, planning to comfort myself with my fingers, but my heart wasn't in it. I wasn't sure I deserved any pleasure, now or in the future.

I sank into dreamland as though falling into a world more vivid than the one I lived in. I dreamed of a glowing white horse, small but full of energy, with no saddle or bridle. She broke a fence with her hooves, and then bucked wildly to throw something off her back. When she turned her head in my direction, I saw fiery red eyes. Sparks flew from stones on the ground each time her hooves struck them.

In the dream, I wondered whether she was a demon horse from a comic book or a horror movie of my youth—the kind of creature that appears to those who tempt fate by playing with ouija boards or magic spells. I liked watching her, in spite of my fear.

When I woke up, I realized that the horse in my dream was one of the few wild animals I had ever imagined in its natural habitat, with no barriers between me and it—or her, the nightmare of legend. She was as different from a domesticated horse as a pet dog is different from a wolf.

I got up when the sky outdoors was still gray, but in winter, that didn't mean it was early. I took a long hot shower in Julia's thoroughly modern bathroom, imagining her enjoying the massage of hot water on her skin after a full day of farm work. My image in the mirror looked healthier and classier than it had the night before.

I dressed in yesterday's jeans and put on the red sweater I had brought with me. My wardrobe was limited, but cutting-edge style wouldn't be appropriate on a farm anyway. *The red sweater is warmer than the one I wore yesterday*, I told myself. *Whether I look good in it is not the point.*

I found Julia in the barn, combing Misty's mane.

"Good morning!" She sounded amused, as though she could guess what I had dreamed about. I could see her breath when she spoke, giving her words the illusion of a life of their own.

The pony had a bluish-gray coat and the long, shaggy mane and tail of her Shetland ancestors. The sounds she made told me that she liked Julia's attention. *Who wouldn't?*

"You want to try it?" Julia handed me the currycomb.

I didn't feel free to refuse. I ran it carefully through the coarse hair, using my fingers too, and Misty rewarded me with a whicker that sounded friendly, although she seemed too restless to stand still.

"That's it. I want her to get used to being handled. It'll make things easier when I put the harness on her."

I could get used to being handled, I thought. *But would I really want a bit between my teeth and a saddle on my back?*

"Chris, you can't spend all day doing that. I haven't collected the eggs yet, and the goats need to be fed. We can take a break at noon. Then we'll talk."

For the rest of the morning, I felt as if I had been subpoenaed to appear in court. *We'll talk*. About what? Would this talk be a lecture or an interrogation?

While I was trying to avoid being knocked down by the goats without running away from them, I saw Misty plunging about in the soft snow. The farm collie was barking and nipping at her legs, and I thought I should intervene. Did dogs usually attack horses? I really didn't know. But then I saw that the two animals were playing a game of feint, sidestep, retreat, and counter-feint. It was a dance or a language that I had never learned. The interspecies friendship in front of me almost distracted me from thinking about Julia.

She lured a goat away from me and then stood beside me, hip-to-hip, and wrapped a shaking arm around my parka-covered shoulders. She wasn't shaking from the cold, and a glance at her face showed me the big laugh that she was barely holding inside. "Come up to the house for some grub, wrangler."

In the mudroom, we took off our boots, coats, mittens, scarves, and hats. In the warmth of the kitchen, I was tempted to keep going by peeling off my sweater and jeans. I decided not to risk being kicked out in my underwear or my skin.

Julia pulled a plastic container out of the freezer and emptied the contents into a pot on the stove. The smells of a savory beef soup wafted through the room. As though saving her breath, Julia wordlessly poured coffee from the morning into two cups and handed me one. "Chris, you obviously needed sleep last night, but now you need to tell me why you're here."

I moved away from her, looking around the kitchen.

"Cream is in the fridge, sugar is on the table. Fix your coffee and then sit down and talk to me. Are you running from the cops?"

I forced myself to sit and look at her. When she was serious, it was hard to believe she was able to smile. "No, they didn't charge any of us." I hoped Julia would feel reassured.

"For what?"

"Julia, it's complicated."

"Cut the crap. I took you in and you owe me an explanation. Is this about Bert's drinking?"

I wanted to jump up and run out the door, but Julia stood behind me, holding my shoulders down. "Let's try it like this, baby. Just tell me what happened."

Tears stung my eyes, and I furiously tried to blink them away. Then the words came.

I don't remember telling her about Bert's rages over my real and imagined disloyalty, our on-again, off-again relationship, her unbelievable, swear-to-God promises, or my stupid hope. The last scene replayed in my mind. I could smell the beer in my hair and feel it dripping off my nose. I could see Bert's teeth and tongue as she yelled in my face, and feel the punches in my back from her playmate and drinking buddy.

"I grabbed a knife," I told Julia. "We were in the kitchen, and I saw it, so I grabbed it. They're lucky I didn't stab them. We're all lucky. The local police came, but they didn't do anything. They laughed."

"Male cops?"

"Yeah. They didn't take it seriously once they knew we were all women." I felt nauseated. My head throbbed.

I knew nothing about handling animals or surviving on the land. After the self-destruction of patriarchal civilization, I would be useless until I learned a whole new set of skills. Now it was clear that I still couldn't stay out of trailer-trash dyke dramas. I just wanted to disappear.

Julia pulled me up from my chair, turned me around, and held me close. "Baby." She poured the syrupy word into my ear. "You'll be all right."

I couldn't stand her sympathy. "I'm not the victim," I reminded her. "I grabbed a knife. I'm not a person who does that. I manage an office now, and I have a frigging degree. Jesus."

I tried to ease myself out of her custody, to no avail. She pulled back to look at me but kept me in a firm grip. "What do you feel so bad about?"

Shame boiled up out of my belly like bile, almost choking me. "I have to go," I babbled. "I just have to go. I'm sorry. This isn't your problem."

I could hardly believe what I saw in Julia's eyes. Amusement, affection, sympathy had all been there before, but now she almost beamed with a kind of predatory anticipation. "Did you really *want* to get busted? Do you think you deserve punishment?"

Yes! screamed a voice in my head. "I don't know," I said. Did I want her to accept my violent streak, thereby showing a lack of class? Or did I want her to demonstrate pacifist feminist values by kicking me out in the snow?

"Yes you do, honey. What do you need to feel before you can forgive yourself?"

"Oh. I see what you mean." I saw the gleam in her eyes. Omigod. I saw her hands itch to help me do penance. It would all be in fun, of course, if a rough game that left real marks could be called fun. I had been warned about Julia, and I had driven for three hours on an icy highway to get here. I couldn't pretend to be shocked.

"Smart girl. If you see what I mean, do you trust me?"

"Yes. Julia, you've always stayed out of the bullshit, as long as I've known you." I remembered her comment about shoveling shit. The stuff she dealt with was bound to be more useful than the waste products of those with nothing better to do.

She pressed her lips to mine in a long, warm, tongueful kiss. I felt myself melting inside. "Do you want me to show you a few things?" Her eyes dared me.

"Yes, ma'am. I do."

I felt as if I had stepped through an invisible door into a world I had been peering at for years, telling myself that what I wanted was impossible. If I had known how easy it was to say yes, I might not have driven Bert crazy by being half-present, never quite there.

"What will you say if you want me to stop?"

"Mustang," I told her. "I'll say that."

"Okay, varmint, I'm the sheriff around here, and you're under arrest. I'm not letting you go until you show the proper attitude. Take your clothes off."

She wasn't holding me. I could have run up the stairs, grabbed my stuff, pulled on my parka, walked out to my car, and hit the road. But I didn't want to. "Really?" I wondered how serious she was.

She grinned. "Really. If you want to play, you'll follow my rules. Unless you'd rather go back to the barn to work. I might make you do that anyway."

I felt strangely free as I pulled my sweater over my head, unhooked my own bra, unzipped my jeans, and wiggled out of them. After I had taken my panties off, revealing the dark triangle of hair between my thighs, my socks followed. When I had neatly folded all my clothes and left them in a pile on her kitchen floor, I straightened up for inspection.

"Nice, baby." She walked around me, casually running a warm hand across my back, over my ribs, across my puckered nipples, and then over my sensitive stomach to my crotch. "Bend over." As I bent forward from the waist, she shoved two fingers into my cunt as far as they would go. I bit down on a squeal.

"Um, you're wet. Good girl. You want me, don't you?"

"Oh, Julia," I groaned. "Ever since I met you."

"Yet you didn't say anything." Her work-hardened fingers stroked my soft, wet channel, almost bringing me to the brink of an explosion. "If you want to be with me, you have to tell me what you want. Will you do that?"

"Yes." Answering her questions was hard. That was obviously the point.

She removed her fingers from inside me, releasing the smell of my lust to mingle with the aroma of the soup on the stove. I had never realized before how pungent and wet and viscous my desire could get. It wasn't just a feeling. It was physical evidence. I could never hide it from her again.

She waved her fingers under my nose to reinforce her message. With her other hand, she straightened me up as though I were her toy. "My belt or my hand?"

I must have changed color as an icy jolt ran up my spine. "You're—are you really planning to beat me?"

"I've got other things too, but I don't think you're ready for them. You're not a very experienced little filly, are you?"

"No, ma'am." I wasn't willing to brag about what I could take. She would find out soon enough.

She ran a hand down my back and then slapped my behind—just lightly, as an appetizer. The slap left a faint echo in my flesh, not enough to reach my awakened clit. I wanted it harder.

"You're not too chicken for a spanking, are you?"

"No, ma'am." I felt as if I couldn't get enough air into my lungs. "Please use your hand, ma'am. It's part of you."

"You have a lot to learn, Chris. Everything I use is a part of me. But I'll give you what you want. You'd better be grateful."

I couldn't help shuddering when she calmly unbuckled her belt, hesitated a moment as though she had changed her mind, and then pulled it through the loops of her jeans and dropped it onto the floor, where the metal buckle thunked on the hardwood. I watched as she efficiently unbuttoned her shirt and shed it like a second skin, shucked her jeans, and stood in a matched set of red satin bra and panties, trimmed with lace.

"This what you want to see? Thought I wore granny panties, didn't you?"

"You look—beautiful, Ma'am." She did, too. The frilliness of her underwear actually seemed to bring out the lines of her lean torso and strong arms. It was like seeing a world-class athlete in a lingerie ad.

"Look fast because they're coming off. I work better in the nude." She removed her last scraps of clothing without wasting a motion. Her breasts were even more impressive than I had imagined, and they were crowned with full brown nipples. Her hips had the sleek curves of a statue.

"You know my hands aren't soft, don't you? The hand cream I use is for healing cuts and blisters, not keeping my skin delicate." She sat on a kitchen chair and beckoned. "Over my lap, my girl."

I stretched awkwardly over her lap, bracing myself with my hands and tiptoes on the floor. I loved the warmth of her thighs and the tangy smell of her armpits.

She ran a hand over my buttcheeks and tickled the crack. "Tough chick with a shank. You're soft and sweet here, though.

Not a hard-ass at all. We need to work on that."

Her hand came down, just hard enough to make a sharp sound. The sting hit a second later and made me clench the muscles in my empty cleft. *Slap!* I squirmed, trying to find a more comfortable position. *Slap! Slap!* The irregular rhythm kept me off-guard as it heated my ass. I heard myself squeak, as though from a distance, but I wouldn't beg for mercy.

When my face was wet with tears I couldn't hold back, she stopped. "That's enough, Chris. You need to know your limits."

Every movement I made echoed in the burning skin of my behind. I rose off her lap awkwardly, grateful for her hands on my arms. "You impressed me, baby, but you're not finished. You got me all worked up."

I could have said the same. My clit was screaming for attention, and I wondered how long I would have to wait.

She stood and held me for a moment, and then squeezed each of my nipples in turn, making me jump. "You're so touchy. I need something to hold you in place. Come with me." She pushed me ahead of her toward the stairs. As I suspected, she herded me into the guest room where the bedding still held the shape of my body.

"Don't you make the bed in the morning? Lazy bitch." I felt mortified. I hadn't really believed I would be coming back here.

"Lie down." I crawled cautiously into the center of the bed and eased myself gently onto the rumpled quilt. Where my bottom touched it, it felt like sandpaper. "Arms up." I stretched my arms up, feeling my lungs expand with my reach.

Something clanged against the metal bedposts, and one of my wrists was securely restrained by something that was lined in soft fabric but not very flexible. Soon my other wrist was in the same predicament. I realized that I was cuffed to the bed.

"I need your tongue," she told me. She crawled over me like

a cougar stalking her prey. When her thighs straddled my ears, she effectively cut off my hearing and forced me to focus on her insistent flesh. I heard her say something, but I couldn't distinguish the words. Her meaning was clear enough. Her wet lower lips and the curly hair surrounding them almost covered my nose and mouth. The smell of her hot musk seemed to fill the room.

Julia's cunt felt like the center of the universe. I stretched out my tongue and took a taste. I tried alternating pokes with the tip of my tongue and broad licks on her slippery folds. I found her swelling clit and lavished attention on it. I began learning her movements: which ones meant "Don't stop," and which ones meant "Slow down" or "Lighten up." Her wavelike motion speeded up when I found a responsive spot, so I tried different ways of licking it. Soon she was bucking in an unmistakable way, and I struggled to hang on, or hang in. My face was drenched in her juice, and I felt honored.

She moved away from my face, leaving it cold and wet. My wrists ached, and I wondered when she planned to release me. Something cool and metallic nudged my cunt-lips, which made the pressure in my wrists recede. I was helpless to escape, and that fact intensified every sensation. I could already feel an orgasm building up in my center like a tidal wave. Her head moved down my body, leaving a trail of hot breath. I felt her mouth on my clit as she pushed the metal object into me. "Oh!" I yelled, wondering if she would gag me for making too much noise.

She raised her head and laughed. "Are you always this loud?"

"Nope," I managed to gasp.

She fucked me deeply and steadily, gradually speeding up. She obviously wanted to know what other sound effects she could get out of me. She twisted the dildo, spiraling it in and out. My sore ass was bouncing uncontrollably on the bed as I rushed toward a climax like a full cup overflowing.

"I didn't say you could come," Julia told me. "You have to ask permission."

"Please!" I yelled. "Ma'am!"

"You need so much training in self-control. Okay, bad girl, go for it."

With great relief, I felt my clit and cunt erupt, sending sparks into my ass and assorted shudders and shivers from my head to my feet.

I was still catching my breath when Julia took my wrists out of the cuffs and lowered them to my belly, where my hands helped settle my churning insides. She crouched over me possessively.

"That's just a taste," she bragged. "We need to break for lunch."

I remembered the soup simmering on the stove and realized I was famished. I remembered that human beings are mammals, with the same needs as the rest. From what I had seen today, play and companionship were no less essential for all beings than food, warmth, and sleep.

"Feel better?" She leaned over me with concern, and gave me a long, wet kiss.

"Yes. Julia, you're something else."

"Are you mine?"

Yes! I wanted to tell her. *Oh, Mistress, put me in a stall in your barn and I won't complain. Take over responsibility for my life, and I'll be yours forever.*

Except that I couldn't be. Somewhere in me was a wildness that could be called out by harassment or by unbearable pleasure. It was like a horse that could only be broken with consent, and then only within limits.

"Yours for now," I told Julia.

"That's good enough, honey," she answered. She lay beside me, and rolled me into her arms. "For now. We'll see."

FANCY PANTS

Roxy Katt

G ert and I stood at the fence, each chewing on a straw, each with a cowboy boot on the rail. We gazed out from under the brims of our cowboy hats and watched Abby, in her fancy new English-style duds, bring old Pie-biter out of the barn for a ride.

"She's really done it," said Gertrude. "She's gone to the other side."

"Yep," I said.

"Why would she do a damn fool thing like that?"

"Too good for the likes of us, I guess. Heard some rich Easterners'll pay good money to learn how to ride, and that's the way they like it done."

"But you're still her girl, ain't you?"

"Yes'm. Leastways, she ain't told me differently...yet."

"This ranch has always been Western."

"I know."

"I mean, it's not like there's any *rules* against English style, but it don't quite fit in, do it?"

"Nope," I said.

"I don't like that foreign English style. Nothin' personal, but it just rubs me the wrong way. I like to wear jeans and cowboy boots and a cowboy hat when I ride. And I like to see other women who ride wear the same thing, more or less. Sturdy girls, you know, big or small, mounted on a rugged, heavy, Western saddle."

"It just seems right."

"Damn straight it does. Now the English style, with that little black helmet and the jodhpurs, well, that's fine for *some* people..."

"Uh-huh."

"But *look* at her. All in bright white, 'cept for boots and helmet. White jods, fancy white blouse with girly frills on the front, white kid gauntlets—you're s'posed to be able to get *dirty* when you're a cowboy, Chris. What's she thinkin'? She's gone lipstick on us. I know she's your girl and all, but I've got to say it: Abby done gone lipstick on us. Double-Q ranch has been Western as long as anyone can remember. Sure, once in a while a dude of one sort or the other comes along in their poncey outfits, but we just smile at them and watch with our boots on the fence railings, suckin' on a piece of straw, and sooner or later they come to see this just ain't the place for them, is it? Nothin' personal, of course."

"Uh-huh," I said.

"But Abby! Why, she's a regular. Been here at least five years..."

"Six."

"...and always in the good old Western style. Now she's kowtowin' to know-nothin' city folk. Next thing you know it'll be 'steeplechase' and 'dressage,' and makin' horses do fancy tricks even a monkey'd turn his nose up at. They bring shame to the animal. Hell, she might as well lace on a corset and some frilly undies and sing with the powder puff girls at the music hall. What's got into her?"

"It's more a matter of what she's got into."

"Huh?"

"Those pants, I'd say."

Gert looked at me for a moment, uncomprehending. Then she smiled a little. "Yeah. Well, that's somethin' else alright."

Abby sure filled out those jodhpurs, I had to admit. They weren't the baggy kind, by the way, but the kind that's tight all the way up. She was one of those short-waisted women with super long legs, powerful thighs, and a big ass shaped like an upside-down Valentine heart. You've probably noticed the type. Her upper body, on the other hand, was slight, small breasted, and seemed almost to belong to a different woman. A smaller woman, like myself. Yessir, she was like a small rider on a big horse, a horse with a big, juicy ass. An ass so full and firm you just had to pinch it—if you dared.

As for me, I'm just kind of small and ornery—although some girls have said I'm kind of cute. Abby was the real looker of the two of us.

"Must have taken her some time," Gert said thoughtfully, shifting the straw from one side of her mouth to the other, "to get her thighs in there."

"Yep." I smiled. I wouldn't have minded helping her into those pants if she'd mentioned it, actually.

Or out.

"Sexy as hell, if you don't mind my sayin' so," Gert added, "but is all that getup fit for ridin'?"

It was funny because Abby was a darned good cowboy and ordinarily looked the part too. She was a blonde with an impressive cable of braided hair; a tanned, freckled face; bold, staring blue eyes; and a big mouth—big in what you might say were the literal and figurative senses—with large, powerful teeth. Those big, beautiful teeth were framed by generous lips, now under deep red lipstick, something I'd never known her to wear before.

"Anyhow," said Gertrude, "she's your girl, you talk to her. I'm out of here. I'm off to the music hall. If'n I wants me a girly-girl, that's where they oughta be. Not on a ranch."

Alone now, I walked over to where Abby was taking some tack out of the barn and getting ready to saddle up old Pie-biter.

"You used to like the Western style," I said.

"Not this again, Chrissy."

"I can't help but feel," I said, stirring the dirt about slowly with the toe of my boot, "that this marks a change in our relationship."

"Meaning?" she said, not looking at me but placing the saddle on Pie-biter.

"I mean, a cowboy is always in charge of her horse. And you and I know, well, you've always been in charge in the hay and I'm not complaining."

"Good. Better not be. And don't you worry," she said, looking back at me significantly from cinching the saddle at Pie-biter's heart girth, "I'm still in charge of my horse; if you know what I mean."

"But with you in those fancified city duds, well, I kind of look at you in a different way. Not a worse way, mind you, just different."

"And just what is that supposed to mean, shorty?" She stood up straight and looked at me.

"It puts me in mind to be doing the riding now."

She set her white-gauntleted hands on her big, pants-busting hips. "Oh, does it?" she said.

I tugged an apple out of my pocket, rubbed it on my sleeve, and examined it closely.

"Something like that," I said. "You know, those fancy pants of yours are pretty hot. You probably need some help getting out of them." I took a bite out of the apple.

"Uh-huh. And you'd like to be that help, wouldn't you, cowboy?"

It sounded like a challenge. She turned back toward Pie-biter and bent over, inspecting a hoof. That sassy little thing, showing off her big ass like that. Abby that is, not the horse.

"It's like this, Abby. You see, I'm right proud that I'm your girl. And I have no complaints about how you ride. Yes'm, I like it that way. But it's like this. I just can't have it said here-abouts that the woman that rides in my saddle is some poncey-assed toff in fancy-pants foreign duds no real cowboy would be caught dead in. Don't get me wrong. I love them pants o' yours. They get me all hot and bothered, actually, but if you're going to be wearing *them* and that girly princess getup, it's gonna be *me* with the reins in her hand. Do you hear? It's just what the interlectuals might say is the semiotics of the situation."

"What?" she cried, losing all patience, standing up, facing me again with her gauntleted hands on her hips as before. "So you want to change things, do you? You're gonna top *me*, are you, shorty?"

I picked up a bit of rope on the ground and began playing with it, innocently. "Me and you have always done it like horse and rider, Abby. We both know which of us is which. But when I see you in that girlie getup, I gotta say, it gets me all hot in such a way as I need to be in charge when I do you. That's the way it is, Abby. You gonna dress like that and I'm gonna take you. And I'd be much obliged if you didn't call me 'shorty' in quite that tone of voice, young lady."

"*Young lady?* What you gonna do, cowboy? Tie me up with that rope?"

"Yep. Then I'm gonna strip them fine pants off your hide and fuck you cross-eyed, woman. And there ain't a thing you can do about it."

I knew she would either take a swing at me then, or laugh. Well, she laughed. Stood there with her hands on her gorgeous hips and her head thrown back, and her glorious big mouth open with all that red lipstick and the big shiny teeth, and she laughed. And that's when I, who've put a bit and bridle on many a reluctant horse, upped and jammed that apple right in her big laughing mouth.

She wasn't expecting that. It shut her up directly. Her eyes rolled like a filly in a panic, and her white-gauntleted hands went right up to the apple and tried to pull it out. But it was stuck in there pretty good. She forgot all about me then, trying to pry a finger in there to get the apple out, bent over a little with her big ass sticking out, and I went around behind her.

I gave her breech-straining backside the smack of her life.

The sound of it echoed over the fields, and, just as I knew she would, she screamed in a rage and put both her hands back there to rub her sore butt.

That was the worst mistake she could have made. Before you could say "Tuscaloosa" I'd bound her wrists behind her with that rope. You should have heard her then, shouting and raging as best she could with that apple stuck in her mouth. She turned and charged at me and would have bowled me over like a bull rolling a gopher except I grabbed both her tits through her fine white shirt with all the frills in front and squeezed for all I was worth.

That stopped her dead in her tracks. She cried out, her head falling back, her knees buckling, her eyes crossing. I let go her tits

and grabbed her shoulders to spin her around. Then I smacked
her ass again.

She bolted, began to run and buck like a horse with a burr
under her blanket. But I chased her around the barnyard,
smacking first one cheek and then the other, making her scream
out her rage and anguish each time in a funny, muffled way. She
wasn't used to that, nossir. She was always the one to do the
smacking and the chasing, but not this time. She turned on me
and tried to kick, but I was smaller and faster, and she didn't
have the balance, what with her arms bound like that. Each time
I got behind her and smacked that ass of hers again and sent her
running.

"I aim to show you, fancy-pants," I said, chasing her around
the barnyard, "that on this ranch you're either a cowboy or a
horse. Your thoughtless change of riding accoutrements, if I may
say so, means you sure don't dress like no cowboy, so you must
be a horse. And since you're such a pretty gosh-darned horse,
I'm gonna ride you. You hear? You changed the dynamic, honey,
and I'm gonna show you how it works."

Tired, confused, her ass sore as hell by then, her strength
began to flag. I took her by the tits again and backed her up
against the barn wall. I grabbed her around the neck with one
hand—not too hard, mind you—and looked her in the eye as I
slowly unbuttoned her pants with the other hand. It wasn't easy.
Those pants were damned tight. She stared back with those blue
eyes wide open, chest heaving, big red lips helplessly stretched to
the limit around that fat apple.

I smiled, still working. "Damn, Abby! I never knew looking
stupid would be so sexy on you."

She let out another muffled cry of fierce indignation as I
switched hands on her throat and began to haul her fancy
britches down. She was too sore and too tired out to resist much

now. Yessir, this horse was about to be broken. She struggled, but I stuck a hand inside her...what the hell?

"Lacy pink panties? I'm surprised at you, girl! You thought you were still gonna ride *me* in lacy pink panties? Now what, exactly, did you take me for? Now that was not necessary. It goes way beyond putting on a show for the city slickers. I know you wouldn't have let them Easterners' hands in your pants, but it looks like you were right pleased for their *minds* to get in there, weren't you? You done let them sissify your imagination, girl. Oh, my, you're gonna git it now. You know what happens to fool girls in lacy pink panties, don't you?"

She groaned and squeezed her eyes shut as I stuck my hand in her girly panties and grabbed a fistful of fur.

I slipped a finger inside her snatch and she trembled. I took my other hand from around her neck and pulled her fancy panties and her pants down to the knees. Lazily, I turned my finger about in her pussy. She clamped her thighs together and groaned, trembling.

"So, missy, you gonna do as I say, or am I gonna leave you out here with your ass and your big hairy pussy naked for the other girls to find and laugh at? Hell. You're so furry down here I wouldn't be surprised if they just shaved you and made a hat out of your pelt. You can wear this silly outfit as much as you like then, 'cause after that nobody's gonna *let* you dress like a cowboy."

Yes'm, this filly wasn't going nowhere without my say-so. I stepped back to look at my handiwork. "I could leave you right now, couldn't I? That would show you. Don't believe me? Listen. I've got some work to do down by Tinker's Bridge. Should be no more than an hour. I'll be back then. Of course, if some of the girls find you before..."

She shook her head desperately and I laughed. I knew what

a blow it would be to her pride to be found like that. "Maybe I should just see if I can find me a pencil and write up a little sign. How about 'free apples'?"

She shook her head desperately, imploringly, and I couldn't help but laugh my ass off.

I began to shuck off my boots and my jeans. "You know what to do, girl. On your knees, now. Git!" She did as she was told. I stepped up to her now in nothing but my hat and shirt. With one expert motion I popped the apple out of her mouth. Her fine red lipstick was running down her mouth with drool.

"Chrissy! No! Not out here. Not out in the open. Someone might..."

"Let 'em. You don't want people to see? You'd best finish me off then before they come. I ain't got nothing to be ashamed of. I'm just watering my horse, is all."

I grabbed her head in both hands, leaned back a little, and pulled her face into my cunt. She must have let go of something inside her then, because she fell into a desperate panic to bring me off, like her very life depended on it. And boy, did that work! I just let her roll her tongue up and down in there, working me into a quiet frenzy.

"You've been needing this a long time, missy, and if I didn't know any better, I'd say it was the very reason—all kind of subconscious-like—you squeezed your big ass into these fancy duds."

But she didn't have much to say. She was chowing down on fresh pussy, pushing her tongue up there as far as it would go, serving my lips with hers as eager as a trout to swim upstream and wiggling twice as hard. She was mine, all right, dying to serve and please me, and she did it right well.

And when I was good and done for the time being, and ready to collapse on the ground and just look up at the puffy clouds go by and think about nothing but how beautiful it all was, I looked down into those big blue eyes of hers and said, "Now, little lady. Do we have an understanding? You can wear that riding outfit any time you like, but just you remember. If you do, you're not the one doing the riding. You hear?"

She did.

TWO FRONTS

Craig J. Sorensen

While the candles still glowed on the cake presented by our cook, Ma said, "Edith, It's a fine thing you've proved you're tough, and that you can ride, but now it's time for you to be a lady."

But my favorite aunt nudged me. "If you'd been born a few years sooner, Edie, you'd have been a rodeo champ right up there with Tad Lucas." Our cook Lucille—Lucy to me—gave me a wink. Now I know that was far from true, but it sure was nice to hear, especially from tough Aunt Dottie, and the grin on Lucille's face was like that pure white icing.

"Now you stop that talk, Dorothy! She's Edith now, and she is gonna be the next queen of the Snake River Stampede."

I doubted that too. Even Eileen Hooker, the first Miss Idaho, and a woman who later caught Darryl Zanuck's eye, fell short at the Stampede contest that same year. And I really didn't want to be the queen, though I'm sure it would have made Ma, who at the age of fifty-five was still one of the prettiest women around, proud.

"You make a wish and blow out them candles," Ma said. I knew my only wish, that my two big brothers would come home from World War II for my birthday, was unrealistic. I blew the eighteen candles out and hoped for the best.

In town, I took it for granted that Matthew Douglas would fill my dance card. We had been predestined—or so our folks told us from the time we were three—to be together. Matthew was going to inherit a nice, small range just down the road apiece. Ma and Pa taught me every angle of the ranch business, and my book smarts with numbers seemed like proof positive that they had made the right choice.

Ever since I had turned sixteen, Matthew and I went to the nearest movie house, about an hour in his jalopy from my house, nearly every week. The way Matthew and I took to fighting during those drives as time wore on just seemed to convince my folks they were right in pushing us two together. It convinced me it wouldn't work, but just like Ma taught me, I put on the airs.

At the dance, after a fight I don't recall the reason for, we split ways and I sat off to the side fuming, while he took up with Rebecca Carlson. Rebecca, with her curly red tresses, bright green eyes, snowy white skin, and hourglass figure, was the girl who should have been Queen of the Stampede.

I stared at the two as they stood in a little too close. I felt frustrated and mad. I felt twinges in my waist work down my legs. I became desperately uncomfortable as I watched the two sway in time to the music

I suppose it's a story unto itself that on one particularly sunny and happy day not long after the dance, we received two telegrams at the ranch. One from an island in the South Seas, one from France. One from the Army, one from the Navy.

It was the one and only time I saw tears flow from my pa's

eyes. Ma didn't cry for days. She sat, hands folded on her lap, one foot slowly pushing that spot on the floorboards where it creaked, slowly tipping the same rocker she'd nursed all three of us kids in back and forth. She stared out across the hard-packed earth in front of the house toward the empty corral where us three kids had learned to ride, and later broke horses. The growing realization that she'd never see either of her boys in that corral seemed to just suck all the life out of her small body.

Life did go on, as it did for so many during those times, but you don't think of the many when something like this happens. You spiral in tight and think of yourself, and those you love. You find things to focus on.

It was a ten-day drive to the railhead to deliver the cattle each year, a trip that every man in the family had taken. Pa had never missed a one since he rode with his pappy. Despite the fact that we had one of the best foremen for a hundred miles around, Pa always insisted on going and taking care of the transaction with that wily old sharp named Chuck. Oh, the stories he told about "brain-wrangling" Chuck.

But this year, with his boys still fresh in the ground, his heart broken, and his will bent like a willow switch, I knew he'd never be able to make it, even if he didn't know it himself.

Lucille was thirty-five years old, part Blackfoot, and hard as a railroad spike. She could ride with the best on the ranch. She understood horses in a way that the men on the ranch, even our foreman Earl, didn't.

Despite her hard edge, she was a handsome woman, and just about every ranch hand that came and went tried to woo her. Every year she had to join the drive down to the railhead to feed the crew and tend to their wounds. "Edie, the only way I can keep them on their side of the camp but not rile 'em against me is to let 'em know I ain't interested. Not just in them, but in nobody."

I only got part of this when she said it.

"Pa, Ma ain't right since Harry Junior and Frank died. You gotta stay with her this year." This was the damnedest argument an eighteen-year-old girl might make to her father, one of the toughest ranchers there ever was, about his wife, who was as tough as him. We didn't get sentimental back then. Hard winter, drive through it. Hoof-and-mouth run rampant, start over. Lose a leg, get another. Hop.

The fact that he bought my argument—that he let his little girl represent the family on the drive—just showed how beat he was. It broke my heart. At first I thought the way Earl so easily accepted me riding along was because of all the hardships the family had taken. Strange, but he seemed almost relieved to have me along.

It was said that Earl once had a small ranch of his own in Montana. Mostly, this was just camp talk, because Earl never said one way or the other. He'd seemed almost to invite me along, so I was surprised when he shouted at me nearly day and night during the drive.

He had me wrangling strays. Every dirty job, he set me to it, and I did them all. Every wrong move of mine, no matter how small, made him snap like a startled rattler. He rode me harder than a fresh Pony Express mount. Earl was famously tough on the hands when they screwed up; I'd seen it plenty of times. Many were the hands that didn't make the grade, and they went on to other ranches. But he was equally loyal and kind when the hands did good.

But it seemed I could do no good.

I was convinced that Earl was just showing that a woman

couldn't handle something like this ride and was exerting his
control while Pa mended his spirit. Maybe Earl just needed to
teach me a lesson.

But the one person in this world I never saw Earl shout at
was Lucille. Some said it was because she was a good cook and a
better healer—worth her weight in gold on the trail. Others said
it was because he was sweet on her. A few even quietly supposed
they were secret lovers. One or two said he was just plain scared
of her.

Seven days into the ride, Earl still shouted orders at me like
I was the worst horse wrangler there had ever been. Even the
hardest, most senior hand on the drive took him aside and tried
to tell him to take it easy on me, that I'd been through enough.

And he came down on my defender as hard as he was coming
down on me. The hands stopped trying to tell him how to
treat me. Little by little, I could tell they were now wrestling
for his place. I think everyone assumed that once we got back,
Earl would be out a job after beating down the spirit of Harry
Senior's little girl.

I'd been in a saddle since before I could remember. Though at
eighteen I weighed barely a hundred pounds soaking wet, I'd
broken horses since before my breasts grew and my hips spread.
I learned how sometimes a horse, on the verge of breaking, will
simply surrender peaceably, while others will squish that final
bit of energy into one last, furious fight. The first one who did
that tossed me like a feather, but I didn't land like one. It took
all my will not to burst into tears, and as Lucy tended my hurt
knee and back, she whispered, "You know, Edie, there's better
ways to come to terms with a horse."

I'd wrangled with the ways of the horse from the outlook
of the rider. Scissoring my tiny legs and clenching my knuckles

white in the mane, rocking my body in time with the horse, I'd try to anticipate where she'd take me next.

Now I was starting to see the same fight from the mustang's side.

My ass was sore from being in the saddle eight days steady, and all I wanted was sleep. But after dinner, as the sun cut low in the sky, I quietly rode back in the direction we came from, not intending to stop for good until I was back at the ranch. Let Earl finish the drive like I figured he must want. He'd proven his point. I'd sooner run than buck.

The hands had spoken of a pond just west of where we had passed earlier that day, and I set out to find it. All I wanted was to wash off the thick trail dust and the sweat. I wanted to be entombed in enough water that my dammed tears would wash clean without being observed even by the critters before I continued back to the ranch, my tail between my legs. I wanted my big, soft bed and maybe a sweet pat on the head from my folks.

The sounds of birds and squirrels chattered through the stand of trees that shielded the pond. I reached it as the sun was beginning to set. It was particularly beautiful, but I thought it felt a lot like that day that the two telegrams had come. I had this feeling of surrender, of broken will. I was not just coming to terms, but embracing the very idea that I should run away, something I'd hated since I was a girl. I pulled my shirt from the top of my jeans, unbuttoned it, and tossed it on a rock. I kicked my boots off and pulled my jeans down to my ankles.

"Sometimes a lady just needs a nice bath."

I crossed my arms over my bra and panties and turned around. "Lucy?"

"Hi, Edie. Or should I say Edith now?"

I let my arms relax. "Edie's fine." Lucy's presence couldn't be more welcome. "Shouldn't you be back at the camp?"

"I think we must of had the same idea." Lucy stripped away her shirt and jeans, and I watched as her skin emerged. I wasn't sure if I should go on, but Lucy's tall strong body was nude within a moment. I suddenly felt safer and removed my underwear. I joined Lucy in the water.

It was chilly, and somehow comforting. I gasped when my upper body disappeared into the softly lapping waves. We exchanged a bar of Ivory soap from my bedroll, and eventually we began to play like kids, splashing each other's faces.

"Lucy?"

"Hmm?"

"What's it like—to be with a man?"

Lucy just shrugged. "Well, it's okay, I guess."

"Are you and Earl lovers?"

Lucy let out a broad laugh.

"I'm betting that's a no."

Lucy paused. "We're not lovers."

The look in her eyes. The way she glanced away from me, then at me, then away. I started to feel this warming, swirling feeling. "You're not too sweet on men, are you?"

"I'm a loner, Edie."

"It's something more."

She simply looked at me. Her jaw gaped for a time. "Don't make a fuss, Miss Edie."

"You don't like men, do you?"

"I like men fine. I like them to ride with, to drink with, and to tell stories around the campfire. I even like to cook for them."

"But there are some things you'd rather not do with them?" My voice came out like a mouse's squeak. It was good that it was a quiet evening.

"Let's just leave it where it lies, Edith."

"You'd rather—be like a man?"

She drew a deep, quivering breath like I'd never heard from this tough woman. "Not at all. I'd rather be a woman, and I'd rather be it with a woman. Clear enough? We best be going." She turned away and started to walk from the water.

As her body emerged, all dark and shiny and warm, the feelings in my waist swirled deeper, harder. The dimple in her lower back, the firm shape of her butt, the strong curve of muscular thighs... There were those feelings I'd had since I was a girl, when I'd watched the pretty schoolteacher, the way her hips swayed when she erased things from the chalkboard. I'd always felt so wrong, or like maybe this was just some idea I was playing with, the kind of thinking a girl does to figure out how things work. It hadn't occurred to me that another woman might feel this way. The feelings I'd had, watching Matthew dance with Rebecca, how my eyes drained down her every time they turned and Rebecca's back faced me, lingered at her exposed shapely calves, and then raced to glare angrily at Matthew.

I'd never seen a thing from Lucy that made me think she might feel like me inside, at least not a thing that I could understand till then. "Lucy?"

She turned her head back over her shoulder, and as I looked in her eyes, a fog lifted from mine. Matthew had kissed me a few times, and the press of his lips to mine did give me a tiny squishy feeling. I'd waited for that feeling to grow. I was sure it was supposed to. Why didn't it grow?

And finally, body cold, buried to the tips of my breasts in this clear pond, I felt it. I knew that even if I weren't in a pond, I'd be plenty wet. I just wanted to touch Lucy a little. Her long black hair was still in the bun she set it to for the trail. "Can I wash your hair, Lucy?"

She bit her lip. "Umm—okay." She walked back in, one arm

folded to her breasts, the other draped over her crotch, until she was submerged again. Her arms relaxed, and she slowly turned around and loosened her hair. I lathered the soap in my hands and began to rub Lucy's scalp, then worked her hair deep in the water. I could feel her body stiffen as I grazed her strong back and ribs while I washed. I could feel that she had stopped breathing. "Edith—Edie?"

"Will you do my hair now, Lucy?"

Lucy took a deep breath and sighed loudly. "Okay."

I released my hair and leaned my head back from an arched spine. But as Lucy began to wash, I leaned forward, forcing her to press closer, to where her hands had to gather my wavy tresses off my skin to scrub them. "My hair feels so grimy, please scrub it good." The feel of her fingers, turning over and over in my hair, knuckles grazing the base of my waist, and then massaging into my scalp, put my hips to blaze.

"Miss Edith. I really shouldn't—"

"Just Edie. Finish rinsing my hair, please?"

"Okay." Lucy tried to keep her hands respectful of my skin, but there was no way she could avoid the contact. The feeling was so strong and deep that I turned around sharp and gripped around her waist like one of those smothering snakes.

"Miss—Edie!" I had never seen more than a nod of propriety from Lucy, but she seemed proper as an old-world lady for a moment. I still felt the way her heart beat, with my small breasts pushed under her full ones. We stood in the cold water, our bodies tight, and we stared into each other's eyes. "Really, Edie, you need to think about this. It's a hard thing to love other women. And me, I'm just a—"

"Are you saying you don't feel stirrings for me?"

"I'm not saying that at—oh—at all." She drew a deep breath and shook her head softly.

"I think you know I have those feelings for you." I slipped my hand down her muscular stomach, into her thick pubic hair.

"Edie, you been through a lot lately." But her hips drifted forward and accepted the way I softly combed her curls.

"Doesn't change a thing." I eased my fingers down and cupped her crotch. "Please, kiss me."

Lucy's arms lay like dead fish in the water as she shook her head with decreasing resolve. "Edie, you should—should think this through." But her hips moved back and forth slowly when I eased one finger into her. She felt so perfect and hot inside.

"Please kiss me."

Slowly her arms crept around me and she opened her stance. She drew her mouth down and gave me a closed-lipped kiss. She pulled back. "Okay?"

"More."

"Oh, Edie."

I pushed my face up to hers and kissed her. I pressed tighter and she moaned as I urged one of her arms around from my back down between my legs. As our mouths explored each other, her fingers slowly traced the outside of my nether lips in narrowing circles until she flicked at the sensitive little arrow at the front. Finally, with my hips nearly forcing down for more pressure, her long middle finger entered me. She swirled my clit with her thumb while the one finger opened me little by little. I'd pushed my fingers in myself before, and it felt nothing like this.

She knew things inside me I didn't know. "Edie, I ain't been with a woman in years."

"How can you bear it?" In the deepening dusk we made love, our hands between each other's legs, our mouths wet and united. I fell limp in her strong arms and entwined my legs around her thighs. She pressed a second, then a third finger inside me and found a rhythm that was so furious I nearly passed out. Deeper and deeper swellings pushed down my waist as I writhed into a deep orgasm. The birds chirped like they were under attack at the depth of my scream.

Lucy carried my limp body from the water and laid me out on a huge rock, still radiating the warmth of departed sun. She kissed me deeply and then lay by my side.

"Lucy, I was running away, going back to the ranch."

"I know. Are you going to keep running?"

"If I do, will you go with me?"

"No, I have to finish the drive. They count on me."

The stars were beginning to blaze in the sky. "I don't suppose I'm needed like that. I'm just along to gather the strays." I laughed a little. "But I won't break."

"Damn it all, where you women been?" Earl walked up with an angry gait as we rode into the camp. I stood down from my horse on this moon-bright night. Lucy eyed Earl, but I held up my hand and she stayed put.

I walked up real close to Earl and looked up. Earl towered over everybody, but especially short little me. "Sometimes a lady needs a bath," I said, and rested my hands on my hips.

Earl folded his arms across his ribs. His jaw set. "When we're out on the trail—"

"Sometimes a lady needs a bath, and I won't hear another word of it, are we clear, Earl Miller?"

Earl squinted; then the slightest hint of a smile cut one side of his thin lips. "Yes'm."

A round, balding man in a big black suit stepped from the office when we reached the stockyards. A huge smile crossed his face. "Well, Earl, you seem to be right on time. Is Harry Senior lagging behind?"

"Harry couldn't make the ride this year, Chuck."

Chuck's eyes widened. I recalled Dad talk about negotiating with Chuck, and I could see that hungry wolf look in his eyes for a brief minute before he eased into an earnest, sad expression. "Never thought I'd see the day. I heard tell about the boys. They was good boys. It's sad that so many good ones gotta go so young nowadays."

"Yeah, it's a shame. This here is Edith."

"Oh, sure, Harry's little girl. You shore are a fine filly, little lady. Spittin' image of your ma." Chuck tipped his Stetson. He turned back to Earl with a bit of a wry smile, dismissing me in turn. "Guess we best get inside and do a little business." He patted Earl's shoulder and began to turn him toward the office.

Earl stopped him and turned back to me. "You do business with the 'little lady' there."

Chuck tilted his head and smiled.

Earl leaned in close to me and whispered. "Edith, there's a reason I'm a foreman and not a boss. I may be tough and know how to ranch, but I ain't business smart like your Pa. Like Chuck. Like you. Do your Ma and Pa proud." He turned and patted Chuck's shoulder. "Good luck, ol' boy."

Within a few years, we weren't driving the stock down by horseback but by truck. I'd lived through a small space in time where the old world butted right up against the new. Two fronts, just like the war that took my brothers.

Lucy was right; these were not easy times to be a woman who loved women. I had to act like Aunt Dottie and Lucy, more interested in the ranch than men. But every night I crept down to the room just off the kitchen.

Lucy quenched the fire that lay beneath my flannel shirts and worn blue jeans. We twined legs, pressed together from hips to faces, lingered on each other's breasts and mouths, keeping our voices down as if there were somebody in the house who really didn't know what was going on.

Back then, there were no real places to get sociable with those who loved their own kind. But after Ma and Pa died, I stopped worrying that loving a woman would lose me the ranch, and worse still lose me Lucy somehow. Lucy moved into the master bedroom. Lucy was my lady, my heart, and my life, then and always.

WHEN THE RODEO COMES TO TOWN

Jove Belle

The bell above the door rang two minutes before closing, as if propelled by Murphy and his damned laws. Ronnie had just cleared away the last of the blue plate special—fried catfish and hush puppies because it was Sunday—and scooted out the back door with a wave goodnight, leaving me to explain that only an asshole shows up this late expecting something to eat.

An F-350 with a built-for-comfort horse trailer, the kind that will hold six horses, all the gear, and even a passed-out cowboy after a rough day, stretched across the far side of the gravel lot. *Rodeo's in town.* I flipped the sign on the door from "open" to "closed."

"Don't forget the lock," a soft voice directed from somewhere behind me. "And the lights."

Suddenly, it didn't seem so late.

"I thought you were out of town." I turned slowly, praying my once-solid knees would hold me. Her voice, like spiced rum dripping with molasses, always liquefied several parts of my anatomy.

"Just got back." Lauren sounded tired, but not tired like she wanted to go to sleep. Tired like she was restless and looking for someone to wear her out completely. "Come here."

I slid the deadbolt in place and hit the light switch. Moonlight streaked through the plate-glass window, lighting the path from me to her. I moved slowly, not trusting my legs, or the shadowed, seductive smirk on her face.

"You're too late for dinner. Kitchen's closed." I tried my best to sound annoyed, but mostly I just wanted to strip her naked, lay her out, and make a feast of her.

"So, you're alone?"

I stared at her lips, ripe and full and begging to be sucked. They were the kind of lips that need to be kissed, the kind a girl like me could get lost in, and Lauren knew it.

"Bryn?" She smiled that private, knowing half-smile that promised she knew exactly what I was thinking.

"Yeah?"

"Are you alone?"

I nodded and sucked air. My brain, too sidetracked by the sight of her, forgot to keep track of silly things like breathing when she was near. Lauren—her long, long legs in faded denim; her dust-covered boots worn for function, not fashion; the curve of her lean body, slight, unpronounced, but unmistakably feminine beneath my touch; the dangerous spark in her eyes daring me to forget the large window that would display our actions to anyone who drove by—overwhelmed me, as always. Six weeks felt like forever when she was gone, chasing the rodeo over the map. And I had stayed here, waiting, eager for her to call, to write, something.

Instead I got nothing. Lauren left me with painful silence and the memories of her sweat-covered body hovering over mine, pushing me higher, begging me to come for her. I should have been mad as hell to have her show up, presumptuous lust in her eyes. I should have held the door open, foot tapping in righteous anger, and sent her away. I should have been a lot of things, but God help me, I was happy to see her.

Lauren pushed herself up off the green vinyl bench and buried her fingers in the short hair at the base of my neck, loosening the braid I'd managed to keep tight through my shift. "I missed you." She exhaled—a hot gush against my neck, in my ear, tangled in my hair, and down my spine.

I melted into her, molding myself to her will. The room spun, or maybe Lauren moved, circling, drawing me around with her. Then she eased me against the edge of the table. The intoxicating mixture of hard muscle and soft girl flush against me, with the rigid table biting into my backside, set my heart racing.

"Did you miss me?" She punctuated the question with a sharp nip, followed by a slow, sensuous lick along the length of my ear.

Did she want me to answer? How could I, with her hands gliding up my legs, under my skirt, smoothing around to cup my ass? So strong, her hands, the flex of her biceps as she lifted me and then roughly set me on the table. She pushed between my knees, and my uniform hiked up, gathering around my waist.

"Answer me, Bryn." Her voice was hard, bridging the gap between love and demand, jarring my vocal chords into action.

"Yes." I'd forgotten the question, but it didn't matter. Whatever she wanted, wherever she wanted it, I wanted to give it to her.

With a half growl, half moan, Lauren looped her fingers around my panties and started their painfully slow journey to the floor. "I thought about you, about the arch of your back." She traced a wet, scorching trail from my neck to the open vee of my uniform collar, dipping her tongue as deep in my cleavage as it would go. The slick glide of my satin panties and her work-worn hands passed my knees and stretched to my calves. "I thought about you, the way you shiver when I kiss you here." She knelt and placed a small, fleeting kiss on the inside of my thigh. The light pressure traveled through my body in a flash of nerves and excitement.

I gripped her head with both hands and tried to pull her closer. God, I wanted her mouth on me, her tongue, liquid smooth and determined, wrapped around my clit.

Lauren's hands flew to mine—panties forgotten, dangling around my ankles—gripping me hard around the wrists. "Careful, Bryn." Her eyes, dark and lust-filled, warned me. She didn't like to be rushed in her seduction.

Something in the set of my jaw, the rise and fall of my chest, the quiver traveling across the exposed skin of my legs, told her I was not ready to lie back and take it. I wanted—no, *needed*—to grind my hips against her face, to force that beautiful mouth of hers where it belonged. My fingers twitched beneath Lauren's grip, and she tightened her hold.

"My rope is in the truck. Do I need to get it?" The slight flare of her nostrils was the only indication that she wanted to do just that as she guided my hands to the edge of the table on either side of my body.

Lauren didn't say "Don't move," but the message was loud and clear. The one time I'd dared to push too far, she'd tied me, face down and spread wide, to the long banquet-style table running the length of the dining room. Unable to move, I'd begged for her merciful touch as she stroked and fucked me to the explosive brink over and over again, only to stop before I could tumble into star-blind oblivion. Then Lauren sent me soaring. The orgasm had ripped through me, drowning reality in a pulsing black sea of "Oh, God" amazement.

When the room had flooded back in a hail of pinpoint

awareness, she had dragged me off the table and pushed me to my knees. In a frenzy, Lauren had crushed me to her even as she fumbled with the zipper on her Wranglers. With her jeans bunched just below her hips, legs straining against the restricting fabric, I sucked her clit, tracing its length with my tongue. Her fingers had gripped my head, pulling my hair in her sharp, rapid rise to orgasmic release. And when she came, exploding in my mouth, Lauren had slumped over me, her body convulsing and quivering as she regained her control.

The memory rippled through me, flooding me with desire. God, I wanted her. But I held tight to the table, knowing she would take me where I needed to go. The promise was in her dark eyes, in her crooked, teasing smile as she moved a chair into position and sat. Her mouth was inches from my aching cunt, her warm breath whispering across my skin, teasing my clit each time she exhaled.

Lauren placed my feet on the arms of the chair, opening me to the cool air and her demanding gaze. "God, I love the smell of you."

I felt wanton and worshipped as she gripped my ass and lifted me off the table, leaving my pussy suspended in front of her face. She didn't suck or lick; she just spread her lips and took me in, holding me in the warmth of her mouth, her tongue spread flat against my clit. Slowly, so very slowly, she circled my singing bundle of nerves, making me quiver with the soft, gentle torture.

"Please," I begged, knowing I shouldn't. Asking for more, begging Lauren to go faster, would only make her slow her pace. I knew it, but I couldn't hold back the whimpering plea.

She pulled back slightly, her mouth gliding away, her lips coming to a light, puckered kiss against my clit as she straightened in her chair. "What do you want, Bryn?" Lauren's lips were swollen, dark like cherry wine, and I was drunk in the moment.

I swallowed hard against the rising tide of anticipation. How long would she make me wait?

"You," I whispered. "God, Lauren, I want you. Please." I held my hips off the table, exactly as she left me when she pulled away. My muscles burned and shook and I needed her.

"What do you want me to do?" She loosened her grip on my ass and drew her index finger between my cheeks, circling with a teasing rhythm against my clenched anus. Pure fire shot through my belly, burning her into me on a cellular level.

"Make me come," I panted, desperate for her.

She pushed into me, the tip of her finger stretching the tight ring of muscle and wrenching a gasp from deep inside me. "How?" she asked with a wicked smile as she wiggled her finger.

I wanted to lower myself, sink onto that wayward, deviant finger, beg her to fuck me until I screamed. If I tried, I knew she'd remove it, stop the delicious, teasing dance inside me. So I held myself rigid, my thighs trembling with the strain, my cunt quivering with warning tremors. She could do that to me, make me come with a look, a carefully placed word, an exhaled breath against my clit. The circling pressure against my puckered opening, stretching me, readying me for more, but denying the promise, was going to make me explode at any moment.

"Do you like this?" Lauren asked as she added a second finger.

"God, yes," I gasped. "Yes, please. More." I eased closer— barely, imperceptibly, uncontrollably closer to her, to the promise of heaven in her touch.

"I should make you wait." She eased out, then in, fucking my ass. "Make you beg." The warm glide of her tongue over the length of my pussy, teasing my clit in time with her thrusts, made me throb, pressure radiating from her invading touch to every pulsing, sobbing part of me. "But I've missed you so much. The taste of you, the sound of you coming in my hand."

My world narrowed to the beautiful, relentless climb toward orgasm. With every word, every touch, she drew me closer. My body screamed, muscles gathering tighter and tighter, clenching and begging. As I sobbed for release, loving her, praising her touch, she thrust into my pussy, filling me beyond anything I'd known before, and sucked my clit between her teeth, flicking her tongue against me in a pounding tempo of sex and need.

The orgasm tore through me, erupting from somewhere deep inside and radiating outward in waves as I collapsed against the hard surface of the table. I languished there, gasping for breath, reconstructing myself fiber by fiber as she stretched over me, kissing me sweetly. First my forehead, then my eyes, then my cheeks, and finally my mouth—a flurry of tender, soft kisses seasoned with her low murmurs of love and devotion.

As I lay there, the room seeping into my consciousness, I ran my hands over her body, the smooth work-worn denim soft beneath my touch. She stayed there holding me longer than usual, long enough to alarm me. Normally she twitched with pent up energy, restless and ready to move on. I struggled out of her embrace and hopped off the table, wiggling my uniform back into place.

"How long are you in town for this time?" I tried to keep my voice casual, like the answer didn't matter. But, of course, it did.

"That depends on you, Bryn." She watched as I straightened my hair and smoothed my skirt over my legs.

"What do you mean?" The low-grade throb in my pussy told me that no matter what the answer, it wouldn't be long enough.

Lauren kept herself stiffly apart from me but took my hand in hers. "I'm tired of the road. Every morning I wake up and I'm alone. You're here and I go crazy wishing I was with you. I'm tired of wishing." There was a slight quaver in her voice as she finished speaking, and she took a deep breath. "I want to stay here. With you."

My knees shook and my head buzzed. "What are you saying, Lauren, exactly?"

She pressed a soft, sweet kiss to my lips. "I'm saying, take me home."

I laughed, a quiet release of the tension and dread that always preceded her departure. She wanted me. More than the rodeo. "Come on, cowboy. Let me show you the way."

She wrapped her arm around my waist, low and possessive, and I led her out the door and into the rest of our lives.

GIRL COWBOY

Charlotte Dare

Lucille had *some* choices. Either sell the small dairy farm she had struggled to manage on her own or hire a stranger to help her keep it up and running. Either way the dream she'd shared with her husband before he shipped off to war would never come to fruition.

"Mornin', ma'am," he said, tipping his cowboy hat. "Name's Del Mather and I'm here on account of your notice at Crowley's Market." He smiled brightly, his baby face a beacon atop a slender lighthouse dressed in a checkered shirt and dusty Levis.

"I just put that ad up no more than a half hour ago," she said.

"I know. I watched you do it and then followed you here, Mrs. Lucille Grady."

Lucille examined him from the weathered, felted wool of his Stetson down to the worn-out boots with shiny spurs that jingled as he fidgeted. "This is a dairy farm. A very small dairy farm."

"Yes, ma'am," he said, still smiling.

"Forgive me, but you look like you belong breaking horses on a sprawling ranch somewhere in Texas."

He hiccupped in a childlike laugh. "Well, ma'am, I do hail from Amarilla and did work the rodeo circuit for a spell, but these days I'm lookin' for any work what I can do outside and with my hands. A very small dairy farm'll do just fine."

Lucille smiled. "I have a fresh batch of blueberry muffins cooling. Have you eaten breakfast yet?"

He looked at the tip of his boots. "No, ma'am."

She watched Del with fascination as he scoffed down his third muffin and polished off a second cup of black coffee. "Would you like a peach, Mr. Mather? I just picked a basket of enormous ones yesterday."

"No Mister—just call me Del, and yes, I'd love a peach."

Lucille selected the largest one from the basket on the windowsill and wondered when this poor fellow last enjoyed a meal. "Here you go."

"Thank you kindly, Mrs. Grady. I better take this with me. Looks like there's a lot of work to be done out yonder. What do you want done first?"

"The milk needs to be bottled and the eggs crated and taken to Mr. Crowley's. I'm already two hours late on delivery again, but he's been understanding."

"Then I better hop to it." Del sprang from his chair, his hat in one hand and the peach in the other.

"Del," Lucille said, tossing him another peach. "A snack for later."

His sweet grin and the ensuing flutter in her stomach unsettled her. Her stomach hadn't fluttered like that since the day she stood at the Altar of Saint Sebastian Church over four years ago and said "I do" to Henry Grady, Jr.

She quickly grabbed a cloth and occupied herself washing the breakfast dishes. No sense wasting any more time wondering about Mr. Del Mather when there were a dozen peach cobblers to make and deliver to Mr. Crowley's before suppertime.

By late afternoon, Lucille looked out the window for Del. He was by the barn hacking overgrown grass, a job Lucille hadn't assigned, but he'd already completed every task she had given him. He wiped the sweat from his brow and then from his neck with a gray handkerchief Lucille assumed was once white. His shirtsleeves were rolled up, an unusual sight since most young men in New England were shirtless by this time of day in early August—not that Lucille was hoping to see him shirtless.

She walked out onto the back porch. "Del, would you make another delivery to Mr. Crowley for me?"

He trotted over to her, blotting sweat from his upper lip with his forearm. He held out his hands to receive the stack of boxed cobblers. "Mmm-mmm," he said, taking a deep whiff. "I know what I'm buyin' when I get my first paycheck."

When he looked up, Lucille nearly lost her footing on the wooden step from the impact of his placid blue eyes. She stepped down to the ground to get a closer look at them.

"You don't have to wait until payday, Del. I saved one for after supper."

A flush lit his sweaty cheeks. "Supper? Oh, no ma'am, uh, Mrs. Grady, I couldn't impose on you for another meal. You been generous enough what with breakfast and lunch."

"Del, three meals are included in your salary. Quite honestly, I can't afford to pay you that much. It's been a bit of a struggle since Henry..." She stopped herself. "So, there you go." She pointed at the boxes in his hands. "Mr. Crowley's customers are waiting for those, and supper is at six sharp."

Hurrying up the steps and into the house, she was surprised

to find a film of sweat glistening on her own forehead. Well, it was awfully hot out.

She busied herself cutting beef into small pieces so her stew would appear meatier than it really was, a trick Henry caught onto after only a few months. Henry—he'd been dead just about eight months now, and she still missed him so. A respectable widow, she was loyal to her husband's memory. The strokes of her knife came harder and faster. Then how come every time she glanced at this Del character she had to force her eyes away from him?

"Ouch," she shouted as the blood pooled in the sliced skin beside her fingernail. She grabbed a dishrag and applied pressure to her gashed finger as she paced the kitchen.

She sat on the parlor sofa and stared at a photo of Henry on the end table, her heart heavy with loneliness. To feel someone's arms wrapped around her once more...

The rumble of the old pickup chugging up the dirt driveway woke her from her nap.

"What happened?" Del asked, staring at the bloodstained cloth around her finger.

She stood up, still a bit groggy. "Nothing. I nicked it starting supper. I can't believe I fell asleep." She swiped wisps of blonde hair off her face.

"Let me take a look at that."

"No, it's okay," Lucille said, brushing past him into the kitchen. "I have to get supper ready."

He gently grabbed her arm and enchanted her with those piercing eyes. "Supper can wait. Let's fix you up first."

Supper can wait? When was the last time a man ever uttered those words?

He opened the bloody rag and examined the wound with slender fingers dirty under the nails. "Where's your first-aid kit?"

"Under the sink."

"That's some nick you got there. You could damn near bleed a pig with a nick that size." He dabbed the cut with Mercurochrome, wrapped it in gauze, and wound it securely with white tape. He looked up and gave her a warm smile. His teeth sparkled without the slightest hint of tobacco stain, and his lips were thin with a rosy shine.

"You don't look like a cowboy," she blurted with a grin.

His warmth faded into a hard glare. "You don't look like a damsel in distress, yet here we are."

She ripped her hand from his. "I told you I didn't need your help. I was okay."

He threw his hands on his hips. "So okay you were just about bleedin' into your own lap?"

A deep breath gathered her composure. "Mr. Mather, perhaps we can get back to our respective duties and meet back at the supper table at six P.M. How does that sound?"

He glared at her stubbornly. "Sounds plumb fine, Mrs. Grady."

He stalked back outside with a toughie's swagger, leaving Lucille in need of another breath.

Glancing out the window, she smiled at Del washing his hands in the water trough and then turned to carefully inspect the supper table. Steam wafted from the stew bowls, while a stack of white bread rested on a plate and apple cider beckoned in condensation-slick glasses. Fresh-cut blue hydrangeas exploding from a vase added a delicate touch.

"Mrs. Grady?" Del's soft voice floated in from the side door.

"Del? Where are you?"

He materialized behind the screen, holding his hat against his chest. "Mrs. Grady, I'm awful sorry about before. I was awful mean to you, and I apologize."

She laughed. "Mean? How were you mean?"

"I called you a damsel in distress."

"Oh, Del, you saved me from bleeding to death, which I was perfectly contented to do for some odd reason. Come on in and have your stew."

They both sat down and began eating silently.

Lucille's eyes darted between Del and the cloth napkin in her lap. What was it about this petite cowboy from "Amarilla" that had her so captivated? "So, Del, what brings a Texas cowboy all the way up to a Connecticut dairy farm?" she finally asked.

As he looked up over the hydrangeas, the hue of the flowers made his eyes pop a heavenly blue. Lucille nearly forgot her question.

"I needed a new start," he said. "I picked New England on account of it's where the folks in England went when they needed a new start. Seemed to work out good for 'em, so I figured I'd give it a whirl."

"The colonists were running away from something, an oppressive ruler trying to tell them how to live their lives."

"Rings familiar," he mumbled.

"Are you running away from something, Del? The law maybe?" Her lips curled with the thrill of intrigue.

He laughed. "I ain't runnin' from nothin', Mrs. Grady. I reckon I'm runnin' *to* somethin'. A life lived my own way."

"What way is that?"

"Just me bein' able to be me."

"That doesn't seem like too much to ask."

"You'd be surprised," he said, spooning in the last of his stew.

"How old are you, if you don't mind me asking?"

"Twenty-two."

"I knew it. I knew you looked young."

"You're young, too, ain't ya?"

"Twenty-five."

"That's young, all right."

"I don't feel young anymore. It's hard to feel young when you're a widow."

"The war?" Del asked.

She nodded. "Henry was a gunner stationed in Belgium during the Battle of the Bulge. Silliest thing, he didn't even die on the front lines. There was a Jeep crash..." She looked away and let out a soft sigh. "I've never talked about it before."

"I'm sorry," he said, and then regarded her with admiration. "I imagine the day he left you was the hardest day of his life." He scratched his curly dirty-blonde hair and pushed away his empty bowl.

She smiled. "Would you like more stew?"

"Oh, no, Mrs. Grady. As delicious as it was, I wanna have room for that peach cobbler you promised."

"Why don't you go relax out on the porch swing, and I'll put some coffee on."

"You sure you don't need no help cleanin' up?"

"Cleaning up?" she repeated, laughing. "Heavens, Del, what are they teaching boys down there in Amarillo?"

His awkward smile tugged at her heart.

"Thank you, Del," she said sincerely. "Why don't you cut up the cobbler? I'm not too skilled with knives today."

Over the next six months, Lucille had several things to note on the kitchen calendar: the Japanese surrender, her fifth wedding anniversary to Henry, the one-year anniversary of his death, and six months to the day since Del Mather and his sunset of a smile appeared at her door.

More than a farmhand, he had become her friend. Lucille had grown to cherish the simple things—having a meal companion just as interested in conversing as he was in eating; evenings on the porch watching the sun dip below the hillside, then later relaxing by the fireplace, listening to *The Jack Benny Program*. She even taught him how to waltz to Les Brown and Doris Day's hit, "Sentimental Journey."

As she wiped her hands on a dishtowel, she smiled at the thought of waltzing eye-to-eye with him after insisting he remove his boots lest he crush her other set of toes.

He walked in the house and kicked the February snow off his boots as he inhaled the robust smell of his grandmother's Texas chili pouring out of the kitchen.

"Unbelievable, Lucille, smells just unbelievably good," he said.

"I'm filling up your bowl now."

"Be right in."

Lucille had discovered two days after hiring Del that he was sleeping up against a rock at the foot of her property. She quickly moved him into the barn loft and then a month later into the spare bedroom.

He sat down at the table, tore into a slice of white bread, and heaved a large spoonful of chili into his mouth. "Now this is the kind of supper that sticks to your ribs on a cold New England night."

"Have I mastered your grandma's recipe?"

"I'll say. You're a fine cook, Lucille. Haven't tasted a bad meal yet."

"Del, we need to talk."

"'Bout what?"

"You."

His skin suddenly went pallid. "What about?"

"How you spend all your time with an old widow. Don't you want to go out and find a girl of your own?"

He dabbed chili sauce from the corner of his mouth with a grave look. "Lucille, I don't know what you're talkin' 'bout. I can't imagine spendin' my time with no one else."

"But you're a healthy, attractive young man. You need to get yourself a girl before all the good ones are taken."

"There ain't no girl in this town or state gooder, I mean better'n you. Heck, in my mind, you're the best gal in all of New England."

She smiled bitterly as she cleared the table. "I guess you haven't been around Crowley's while they're gossiping about me."

"What do you mean?"

"It's rather obvious, Del. A young widow moves a hand-some farmhand into her house? Oh, the gossip doesn't get much juicier than that."

He got up and brought his bowl to her at the sink. "Why didn't you tell me sooner? I'm goin' to get a room in town tomorrow."

She turned to him. "No, you're not."

"But Lucille, I can't have no one talkin' like that about you."

"Del, I'm no damsel in distress, remember? I don't care what people are saying. They're still buying my milk, eggs, and cobblers. So they shoot me the stink eye in church? That's why I stopped going."

"Oh, now, Lucille, I can't stand by and let these people smear your good name. It just ain't right."

She looked at him squarely in the eye. "There's a way to shut them up."

"What? How?"

She wiggled her eyebrows.

"What? You don't mean marriage," he shouted. "Why, Lucille, we ain't even kissed."

She leaned in and did what she'd wished Del would do to her practically since the day he appeared on her doorstep. His lips were soft and warm and sent a tingle of warmth throughout her entire body.

He threw his arms around her and nearly lifted her off the floor, surprising her with his strength. She whimpered with desire as she began running her hands down the back of his sinewy body. She pressed herself against him, feeling through her thin sweater the cold steel of his belt buckle on her stomach. As he backed away slightly, her grip around his neck grew tighter.

"Del, would you mind if we skip the cobbler tonight?" Still kissing him, she led him toward the stairs, up to his bedroom.

He gently lowered her onto his bed and began kissing her deeply, more passionately than she ever dreamed it would be. Was it ever like this with Henry? She couldn't remember.

"You're the most beautiful woman I ever seen, Lucille," he said, drowning her in his liquid blues. "I would love to make love to you."

The gentle stroking of his fingers across her cheek and weight of his body awakened a frightening, powerful desire in her.

"I'm in love with you, Del. I know I probably shouldn't be, with Henry gone just over a year now, but I can't help myself. I just want you." Her body writhed longingly beneath him.

"I love you, too, Lucille, so much sometimes it hurts."

She grabbed his head and kissed him hungrily. "I want to be close to you, Del," she said in a breathy whisper.

He kissed her neck as he slowly unbuttoned her dress. A delicate moan escaped her lips as his gentle hands caressed her breasts, his tongue titillated her nipples. She pulled the tail of his shirt out of his waistband and stroked his skin.

"Your back is so smooth and soft," she whispered. "Can I feel the rest of you?"

At that, he leapt up and turned off the light, leaving the shaded room in complete darkness.

"What are you doing?" she asked.

"I heard that sometimes girls get embarrassed the first time," he said, fumbling with the zipper on his jeans. "Just shut your eyes and enjoy it."

She shivered as she felt the slow, sensuous penetration. She tried to be quiet like a proper lady, but the intense pleasure forced moans and whimpers from her lips in spite of her efforts. His thrusts increased in strength and speed as her moans grew louder, and soon she was calling out, "Del, Del, oh, Del," in a whirlwind of ecstasy until she shuddered in glorious release.

Afterward, she lay in his arms, spent, trying to catch her breath.

"Del, why didn't you take off your shirt?"

"Didn't seem like there was enough time."

"Take it off now."

"It's cold. I think the fire went out downstairs."

He sprang from the bed, stumbled through the dark bedroom, and disappeared downstairs.

Lucille lay there, still quivering from the pleasure of his touch, listening to him move the screen in front of the fireplace and toss in a log. The fire popped and crackled. She smiled. It seemed whatever Del Mather touched roared to life with boundless intensity.

But what was taking him so long?

"Del, aren't you coming back?" she asked from the stairs.

"Why don't we have our coffee in front of the fire? It's nice and warm now."

She buttoned herself up, slid into her slippers, and headed for the kitchen. After the way he made her feel, making him a pot of coffee was the least she could do.

They continued making love regularly and in the dark. Although Del physically satisfied Lucille to the point where she could think of little else during the day, she grew frustrated with not being able to touch him or feel his skin on hers while he carried her to the heights of pleasure.

As she lay in his arms, she made an idle threat she had no intention of following through with. "Del, if you don't let me touch you, I'm going to stop letting you touch me."

She felt his sigh through his chest. "Don't say that, Lucille."

"But Del, I'm just crazy about you, but I don't feel like I'm getting all of you. I'm tired of being made love to by a plaid work shirt."

He huffed. "*I'm* makin' love to you, not my shirt."

"I just don't understand it. Most times Henry would be naked before he reached the foot of the stairs."

"I ain't Henry," he growled. "And I'm sick of talkin' about Henry and lookin' at his picture. I'm me, Lucille, ain't that enough?"

"Of course it's enough, Del."

Seized by curiosity, she even surprised herself when she grabbed between his legs. Nothing was there, at least nothing she could feel. Del scrambled to his feet but in the dark lost track of the firm rubber appendage hiding at his side.

Lucille found it and shrieked like a banshee.

Del switched on the light, his hands trembling. "Lucille, I'm sorry. Stop screamin'."

"What the hell is this?" she yelled and threw it to the floor.

"Lucille, let me try to explain."

She pulled the covers up to her chest. "Please, Del, please explain to me what the heck is going on."

He paused, rummaging for words. "Do you know what my name is?"

"It's Del Mather. Now what kind of game are you playing with me?"

"I'm not playing any game. My legal name is Della Marie Mather."

"What?" she asked, hearing Del perfectly. "What are you saying to me?" she insisted, holding back a torrent of emotion.

"I'm...uh, I'm not a man, Lucille. I'm a..."

"You're a girl," she screeched. She leapt out of bed, dragging the linens with her like a protective shield while running for her own bedroom. "Oh, good Lord, how could you do this to me? How could you trick me like this?"

He followed, close on her naked heels. "I never aimed to trick you, Lucille. This is who I am, and I just happened to fall in love with you."

"Oh, dear God." She collapsed onto the bed in a fetal position and bawled.

"Lucille, don't cry. Please believe me. I didn't mean to trick you. I just didn't know how to explain myself to you." Del gently touched her side.

"Don't touch me. Leave me alone."

Lucille lay twisted in the sheets, sick with confusion, hoping the tears pouring onto her pillow would wash away everything she loved about Del Mather. She listened as Del gathered his jingly boots and floated down the staircase like a ghost. How could this have happened? How could the first drop of happiness she had tasted since Henry received his marching orders nineteen months ago end like this?

The sound of Del's boots clopping out onto the front porch

impelled her. She hurried down the stairs and stood, pulling on her robe at the open door. "I don't understand, Del," she said with quiet dignity.

Del shrugged. "I'm a girl and a cowboy. It's just never been my dream to have a husband and kids."

"But girls aren't supposed to love other girls that way."

"I know...only boys get to." Del looked down at her masculine outfit. "Sometimes I think I'd like to wear somethin' pretty, but I'd rather have a pretty girl. So I made my choice." She spread her arms apart like an eagle's wings and then let them drop by her side.

Lucille searched Del's face, desperate for something to hate, but her feelings for this girl cowboy were as strong as they had been before the revelation. She sighed bravely. "Take care of yourself, Del."

"I intend to."

At the bus depot the next morning, Lucille scanned the counter for a felted wool Stetson and a plaid cowboy shirt, listening for the jingle of spurs across the wooden floor. Her heart was racing and her feet felt too fat for her shoes in the sweltering station. What she was doing there, she didn't know. She just knew she had to look into Del's eyes once more.

"Del," she shouted as she caught her coming out of the men's restroom.

Startled, Del dropped her satchel and bus ticket by her feet. As she bent to pick them up, Lucille hurried over to her.

"Hello, Lucille," Del said humbly.

"Where are you going?"

"New York City. Ain't my first choice, but I reckon it's where I got the best chance."

She studied Del's delicate features, aware of her natural

beauty for the first time. "Del, I still don't know what to say to you."

"I know. Don't know if I would if I was in your shoes neither. Lucille, these past eight months have been the happiest of my life. Even though I'm a cowboy at heart, I enjoyed tendin' your dairy farm." She looked down at her worn boots and muttered, "I hope you don't hate me too much."

Tears pooled and began spilling down Lucille's cheeks. "I don't," she whispered.

"Well, I guess I better get to boardin' my bus."

"Don't," she said as Del was about to leave.

"Whudja say?"

She sniffled, took a deep breath and spoke softly. "I said don't, Del. Don't leave."

"But I'm gonna miss my bus."

Lucille chuckled through her tears. "That's the point." She gazed into Del's glassy, bloodshot eyes. "I don't want you to go to New York City."

Del looked around the station. "Lucille, I swear I love you more than I ever loved anybody in my life. And if I had my way, I'd spend my life with you on your dairy farm, eatin' your stews and makin' love to you till you can't breathe. But I gotta be who I am. If it means I gotta be on the move for the rest of my life, leavin' people I love, then so be it, but I can't stay nowhere I can't be myself."

Lucille smiled, drawing circles on the dusty floor with the tip of her shoe. "You wouldn't be the person I fell in love with if you did."

Del took Lucille's hand, and, as they left the station, placed her bus ticket on a hobo curled up on a bench by the door.

AN IMMODEST WOMAN

Elazarus Wills

The abducted dog had thrown up on the front seat a hundred miles to the north, which was why the windows on the pickup were rolled all the way down. The smell lingered despite Luce's best efforts with tepid bottled water and paper towels. Now Bongo, his border collie eyes looking apologetic, was whining softly in a tone that meant a visit to the side of the road was needed.

After two years, Luce and Bongo understood one another. Even though the dog technically belonged to Janice, whose ownership of him predated their relationship, Luce was sure, given the choice, that Bongo would have chosen her. She had not given him that choice, just packed him into the truck with the rest of her belongings at two in the morning. Let Janice get another dog. If Luce couldn't retrieve her heart, she would at least have Bongo. Possession was nine-tenths of the law.

She checked the mirrors and slowed down gradually, mindful of the beat-up horse trailer behind. There were no other vehicles visible in the several miles that she could see in each direction. No signs of life at all. The two lanes of alligator-cracked asphalt were as straight as if the builder had been guided by a string stretched taut from Nebraska south to the Oklahoma state line. Luce's destination was a ranch outside of Santa Fe, but in traveling from job to job she had always kept to back roads, avoiding the quicker and somehow lonelier Interstates, places where the world revealed itself as bad-tempered and in a hurry to get nowhere as fast as possible.

Luce McCallister, Bongo, and her Appaloosa cutting horse, Eleanor Roosevelt, were about two-thirds of the way down that string, heading south, when they pulled over so that Bongo could pee. It was mid-September and the prairie was dry, with an electric smell to the air as if the memory of rain hadn't yet disappeared entirely. Luce breathed deeply and brought the truck to a halt where there was a graveled area in front of a gate set into the taut barbed wire and steel fenceposts that paralleled the west side of the highway. A variety of beer cans and potato chip bags littered the nearby weeds where they had been propelled by the wind, giving evidence that others had parked there. To stretch their legs before Oklahoma; to let their kidnapped dogs pee; to take their old horse out of the trailer for a few minutes; to wonder if breaking off a love affair by fleeing in the dead of night wasn't a cowardly act?

Luce realized that her own bladder was pressing at her, so while Bongo selected just the right clump of rabbit brush to relieve himself on, she lowered her jeans and squatted alongside the horse trailer, putting it between herself and the empty road. She felt a little silly since she could have done it in the middle of the highway in perfect privacy, but she was a shy person even when she was alone. The shadow of the trailer and the snuffling of Eleanor inside comforted her. She relaxed and watched a small dust devil, a micro-tornado all of six or eight feet high, weave around out in the dry grass a couple of hundred yards away.

A skinny jackrabbit emerged from the brush and froze into place staring straight at an oblivious Bongo. There was a black spot on the horizon—squarish—a house out there? Beyond the gate, twin tracks wove thorough the grass and sage in the direction of the structure. Might be an old abandoned homestead built back before the early settlers had understood that this landscape was entirely alien from Ohio or Illinois.

Luce wondered what Janice had been thinking a few hours before at the ranch at Jackson Hole, awakening to find the bed and rambling house empty of life, woman and dog gone. What had she thought as she read the three-sentence note on the table in the kitchen? In her kitchen that cost more to build than Luce had made in the previous four years. Luce imagined beautiful, blonde Janice going out to the horse barn and the covered arena that Luce had designed, looking for her. Hoping that she had misread the note.

You don't own me. I own me. Bongo will be happier too. Luce hadn't signed it. She had written the note a half dozen times, tearing up each one. They had all included the word "love." *I love you more than… I love you but…* Love had to be taken out of the formula for leaving. As if it could be.

Luce had gotten Eleanor out of the trailer and was walking her up the narrow shoulder of the road when she heard the faint sound of a motor. Nothing was visible on the highway, but after a while she realized that the sound was coming from the west. She carefully got astride the smooth back of the horse to gain a little elevation, Eleanor patiently allowing her to use her mane for a handhold.

It was a four-wheeler, its small two-stroke motorcycle engine growing louder as it approached. The single rider was wearing a white, billed cap. Bongo, his urgent business finished, finally noticed and barked once, looking over at Luce for direction.

"I see him," Luce said, and Bongo sat down to wait.

As the little ATV grew closer, a plume of dust drifting away behind it, she saw that the rider was a woman, a conclusion not based on clothing, jeans and shirt, but on something ineffable. An attitude. A carriage of the body. The figure waved a gloved hand, and Luce waved back and slid off of Eleanor.

The ATV pulled up behind the gate, and a tall, narrow woman got off. Her dark brown hair, with a sparkle of silver strands, was woven into a single braid that descended halfway down her back. She undid a padlock, dragged the wire and steel stays back, stepped through, closed the gate, and relocked it, leaving the vehicle on the inside. That seemed a little odd.

"Hey," the woman said, removing her cap. Slapping it against one thigh resulted in a little puff of dust. Even her voice sounded dusty. "How ya doing?" Her forehead was slightly pale compared to the lower areas of her face.

"Good," Luce said. Bongo walked over and sniffed at the woman's pant leg.

"Nice-looking horse you got there."

"Eleanor Roosevelt's pretty old," Luce said.

"Not so young myself." The woman grinned, and it was like someone had turned the sun up a notch. "Sometimes older can be an improvement. Me, for example. I'm not as stupid as I used to be." Her eyes showed amusement; her face showed long hours outdoors and a history of laughter. As for age, it was hard to judge; Luce guessed that she might be in her mid-forties.

"There are compensations." Luce took Eleanor's halter and began to lead her back to the trailer.

"That there are."

The woman stood still and quiet while Luce got the horse back into the trailer, checked the hay bag, and gave her a couple of scoops of grain. When Luce was latching the trailer, she saw that the woman was squatting and rubbing Bongo, who leaned contentedly into her.

"Real nice dog," she said. "Bet he's good around the cattle."

"Yeah, Bongo's not too bad." Luce found a pack of gum in her front pocket and offered the woman a stick. She took it. Luce unwrapped one, popped it into her mouth, and began to chew. She waited.

"The thing is, I was wondering if you could give me a ride into town," the woman finally said. Luce looked pointedly at the ATV. "It's forty miles. My ass'd be dead in twenty on that. My truck's in Mazurton getting fixed."

"I'm Luce McCallister, coming from Wyoming. Going to New Mexico." Luce held out a hand. "Happy to give you a lift."

"Happy to get one. And hello Luce McCallister, my name's Eileen Starling. I take care of some cows my brother owns."

Luce explained her job of training horses and designing and building equine set-ups for yuppie New Westers.

"Sounds real interesting except for the people," Eileen commented.

"They can be an issue. The horses never are," Luce said, thinking of Janice, who couldn't move past her money and sense of entitlement. *Thinking of Janice naked and laughing in the loft with a view of the snowy Tetons.*

"Bongo puked on the seat on your side, and it's still a little damp." Luce opened the passenger door, retrieved an old work jacket from behind the seat, and spread it out.

"That'll work fine. I've had worse in my truck. Newborn calves with the scours," Eileen said, and slid in, allowing Luce to shut the door for her. Luce saw the quick smile, mostly in the eyes. *Amusement?*

Once they were moving down the road, Bongo riding bright-eyed between them, Luce took the time to study the woman more closely. She was actually quite striking, beautiful even, with large green eyes that matched the Irishness of her name. This combined with prominent cheekbones and full, lipstick-free lips to give Luce a sudden rush of attraction. She could imagine kissing this woman. *So different from Janice.*

"What are you thinking about?" someone asked. It was Eileen, regarding her with those eyes. "Me, I was wondering if I could buy you lunch when we get to town. It'll be that time of day when we get there."

"Oh." Luce felt a warmness move over her face. "That would be nice. Actually I didn't have breakfast, only coffee." *And she had wanted to put some distance between herself and Janice, as if she felt her lover had the power to draw her back if the number of miles between them were not enough.* She glanced at her own face in the rearview mirror. Thirty-eight years old, worn gray Stetson pulled tight over a short mop of coarse blonde hair. A plain face, she thought.

"So what were you thinking?" Eileen asked.

"Makeup. I was thinking about makeup," Luce said. "How a lot of women feel like they have to put on a mask with all of it." *And how some women are perfect without it. How eye shadow could equal desecration.*

"I've never thought too much about it," Eileen said. An old Volkswagen Beetle passed them heading north, and she leaned out the window and waved. "Someone I know."

"I have always resented it," Luce said. A white-on-blue sign announced that trash on the next two miles of highway was being picked up by the Mazurton Community Methodist

Church, a job she imagined didn't have to be done very often.

"Men are silly, and women encourage them," Eileen said. "I used to drive my mother crazy. Now she's given up and accepted that I'll never be anything but what I am. A permanent tomboy. She should talk. Hell, she's done the same stuff that I do her whole life, only she had to do it in a dress."

"I guess I could be called that too. A tomboy. Tom-woman. A boisterous and immodest woman. I looked it up once. A woman that some men, and some women, don't approve of." Luce stroked Bongo and was startled to encounter Eileen's hand. A couple of late season grasshoppers bounced off of the windshield. *Janice couldn't survive without blush and lipstick.*

"A woman that doesn't give a shit," Eileen said, and laughed in a voice that sounded like singing. The two women rode along in a comfortable silence for a while, petting the dog, Luce enjoying the occasional touch of Eileen's hand.

"It's right up ahead, don't drive on by."

"What?" Luce said automatically, startled out of her personal quiet place.

"The town." Eileen lifted a hand to the west where there was a line of trees, two white-painted water towers, grain elevators, and a discernible roofline or two.

Luce came to a near stop to make the turn onto the gravel road that led into town, going down into a shallow gully and underneath an old iron and concrete railroad bridge. Apparently Mazurton had been built along the tracks and the highway had come later. The trailer banged and rattled on the washboard surface.

The town could be taken in with a sweep of one's vision, three long east-west streets bisected by a dozen or so shorter ones going north-south. The block-and-a-half-long business district was paved with asphalt but appeared to be the only street in town that had been blacktopped. It also had sidewalks. The open prairie was just a few hundred feet from any point within the little town.

"Welcome to the big city," Eileen said. She waved her arm again, and Luce saw the café. "Breakfast and Lunch," the lettering painted onto the storefront's plate glass windows stated. There were three other vehicles, all pickups, parked in front of the café. Luce drove past the restaurant and parked the truck next to the curb. There were no parking spaces marked anywhere on the street.

Eileen got out quickly and came around to the driver's door. "My truck's right down the street at the garage. I'm going to walk over there and get it before he heads home for lunch. Go on in and get a table and order me an iced tea."

"Yes, *dear*," Luce said, an acid edge to her voice. She was immediately embarrassed. It had been an automatic response. She had spoken to a stranger as if she were the overbearing Janice.

"Darlin'," Eileen said.

"What—" Luce could see only green eyes and those lips.

"In Kansas we say *darlin'*," Eileen said, her hand on Luce's bare arm. "Or maybe it's just me that says that." And she leaned in and kissed Luce on the mouth. The kiss was more than a peck and less than a sexual act; a soft, full contact that lasted just long enough to communicate something clearly. "Just so you know," she said, and turned and walked away. It took a moment for Luce to gather herself enough to take her next breath.

Luce went into Breakfast and Lunch and ordered coffee with real cream and honey—and an iced tea. The flavor of the kiss hadn't diminished. *Darlin'*.

The waitress was a robust woman in her early sixties. "There'll be two of you then? You known Eileen for a while?"

she inquired, delivering a pebbled plastic glass full of water and crushed ice. "I'll get her iced tea and the coffee."

"We sort of belong to the same organization," Luce said. She knew that the woman couldn't have seen the kiss, had just seen them drive by together, so the information implied in her inquiry must be local knowledge.

"That's real nice," the woman said. "Eileen needs to have more friends come and visit. I worry about her, being out there by herself all the time. You gonna be here for a few days?" There were a half dozen other people in the restaurant, but they hadn't interrupted their conversations when Luce had come in. Still, she had a suspicion, an almost *knowing*, that she was being focused on.

"Came to stay for a while. Maybe a month or two." Luce lied easily as she saw a big four-wheel-drive Dodge pull up out front with Eileen at the wheel. "I even brought my horse and my dog."

"Two useful things to have in this country," the woman agreed, also seeing Eileen and going to get the tea and coffee.

Eileen came in, making the pair of sheep bells hooked to the front door clang briskly. Several of the others, both men and women, greeted her by name as she passed. She sat down, putting her hat on an empty chair just as the beverages arrived.

"Hey, Jewel. Your timing's always perfect," she said.

"Morning, Eileen," Jewel said, order pad in the palm of her hand. "Your friend was just telling me she was planning to stay a while."

"Could you make us two chicken fries with mashed and the slaw? Extra gravy on the side." Eileen took a swallow of iced tea and looked at Luce, who nodded. It was exactly what she would have ordered. "Hell, she even brought her horse,"

Eileen drawled. "Lady shows up with her horse, you know she's serious." Jewel's face looked a little flushed, and she took the order over to the open kitchen behind a long counter.

"She's the waitress, the cook, and the owner," Eileen said. "I sell her the beef she uses. We do the butchering right here in town."

"You always kiss women traveling through?" Luce said.

"There ain't that many traveling through. Fewer that stop."

"How did you know?"

"I didn't—until you didn't slap me and drive away." Eileen grinned, interlaced both hands behind the back of her head, and arched her back in an exaggerated stretch. "'Course naming your horse Eleanor Roosevelt was a pretty good clue."

"Well, she sort of looks like Eleanor Roosevelt, more when she was a foal," Luce said.

"Now you're gonna have to come keep me company back at the ranch," Eileen said.

"I am?" Luce's breath was coming a little fast. Those green eyes.

"No choice now that you've told Jewel. Everyone in town will know you've come to do unspeakable stuff to poor defenseless me. Don't want to be a liar do you?"

"No—" And it would put even more distance between herself and Janice. She imagined a letter she would write from New Mexico. *The day I left Jackson, I met a wonderful woman in a little town in Kansas. I spent the night with her...*

The little ranch house was surprising, a mix of passive and active solar design embedded into a gentle fold in the prairie. Limestone walls and south-facing glass, a roof covered with red ceramic half-pipe tile, and solar panels.

"I used to teach in the natural sciences at the university in

Lawrence," Eileen said as she opened a door. "After twenty years I decided to *do* instead of teach."

Bongo led the way into the house, which was sun-filled and mostly one large space containing open sleeping loft, living area, and kitchen. The walls were almost entirely covered with bookshelves. Through the south-facing glass she could see Eleanor Roosevelt wandering around in the grassy paddock where they had put her, sharing the space with a dozen black Angus heifers.

"This is really something," Luce said.

"And you thought I was inviting you to my hantavirus shack." Eileen laughed, walking through the house and opening French doors onto a patio shaded by vine-covered framework and slats. "Welcome to Kansas, Dorothy."

"Well, I was thinking something more rustic," Luce said. "But I guess I can make do."

"And now that we're alone…" Eileen turned, unbuttoned her shirt, and took Luce's hand. The second kiss was better, if less of a surprise, than the first.

The flesh on Eileen's belly was brown and taut. In the leaf-mottled sunshine, Luce could make out the line of a scar a few inches to the right of her navel, just a faint white mark about the length of the width of her hand. Under the touch of Luce's fingers a faint ridge could be felt. There was another, similar scar on her left breast. Luce kissed all along it, knowing that she was posing an unspoken question. Eileen stretched her arms to hold onto the sunshade supports above while she stepped out of jeans and panties.

"Long story," she whispered as Luce knelt.

"We all have one or two," Luce said, and kissed her stomach and the point of each hip. She massaged Eileen's firm-feeling butt with the palms of her hands and ran her cheek down a length of smooth, muscular thigh.

"Yes—we do." Eileen groaned, writhed, and stretched. "I'll give a short version."

"I'll keep you motivated on the succinct part," Luce said and kissed Eileen's clit, which was flushed, engorged, and visibly offering itself.

"Here goes—" A gasp through clenched teeth. "I was married once, in Lawrence. Now I'm not."

Luce slid her tongue inside.

"I didn't love him, but I thought I did."

Lips kissed inner thighs; three entering fingers, and then four, bunched. Luce's breath warmed Eileen's navel. "I thought that he was a good person. He wasn't."

Luce slowly stood while keeping her fingers in place, deep inside and moving. She kissed and nibbled as she moved upward, nudging aside the chambray shirt, pausing to sample the flavors of Eileen's flesh. Salt and passion. She smelled like earth, the prairie—sage and a breeze from the southwest.

"There was someone else—a student—a girl—a bad idea." Eileen was shaking by the time Luce reached her breasts, bra lifted above them. They were beautiful, moon-round with nipples framed by wide scarlet-sienna areola. Luce drew the whole of one into her mouth and held it temporary prisoner between her teeth while her tongue caressed the apex.

"He discovered it, and instead of just feeling betrayed, he had to have revenge." The breast scar again. The slash had been deep and clean. Luce felt her own breasts ache in sympathy. There was a second, smaller scar on the right breast, barely visible, about an inch wide, the width of a narrow plunging blade.

Eileen's nipples were erect and a fine network of veins was visible, pulsing below the surface of pale sun-protected skin.

"He had a knife and he cut me."

"Oh, my God," Luce whispered, and kissed her neck, moving

from left to right. She covered Eileen's mouth with her own while the fingers of her right hand continued their penetration. Her other hand held the base of the long braid like a traveling staff, or a rope that anchored her need. When Eileen came she pushed away, and with the knuckles of one hand between her exposed teeth, she sank to her knees and keened. Luce followed her down, keeping one vibrating hand cupped over her sex through the second wave. After a while Eileen staggered to a chaise lounge and sprawled on her back.

"Oh, my God is right, darlin'," she gasped. "I think She may have just dropped in for a visit." Luce sat down next to her on the flagstone and laid her head on Eileen's stomach. "But his attacking me changed my life for the better."

"Made you meaner and stronger?" Luce murmured into Eileen's navel.

"No, it made me realize how dumb and cautious I was. And I decided that for the rest of my life I was going to do exactly what I wanted to do."

"Which is live alone forty miles from town in the middle of nowhere?"

"Yes, ma'am. Just down the road from where I grew up," Eileen said, stroking Luce's hair. "And after a ride, dinner— probably just a salad after that late lunch—and a shower, what I'll want to do is eat you until you say my name like you mean it. Really fucking loud."

An hour before sunset on the prairie was a gorgeous time. It was a stage-set riot of sepia tints, blood reds, and flaming siennas and ochres contrasting with blue-purple shadows. Luce rode Eleanor Roosevelt, who uncharacteristically kept attempting to break into a gallop, while Eileen rode a gelding, seeming almost a part of her mount. Luce watched her closely and guessed that she must be controlling the horse through pressure from her pelvis and calves, but it was undetectable; there wasn't much use of the reins. It was as though horse and woman had become a gestalt, transforming into a single woman-horse entity.

They rode a mile or two out from the house to an old buffalo wallow that was now a bentonite-sealed pond, shaded by a trio of young Fremont cottonwoods and circled by tracks of not just horses and cattle, but many deer and antelope.

They dismounted and sat, listening to frogs and crickets, and Luce told Eileen about Janice. The woman she had thought she loved, *did* love, but who would not accept love without submission. Without possession. Who was so damaged as to be incapable of believing that anyone cared about her separately from the wealth.

"And I had to learn the difference between generous and controlling," Luce said. "I was ashamed that it took hard effort to pack my truck and just drive away. I still am."

"What are you, twelve?" Eileen had taken a joint from her shirt pocket and lit it with a kitchen match ignited by a flick of her thumbnail. "Didn't you state your own terms? Define the borders?"

"Janice is hard to talk to, but she *knew* she was making me miserable. I cried all the time," Luce said defensively. "And I never cry." Bongo laid his head in her lap and looked concerned.

"So you took it and took it until one day you decided that you weren't gonna take it any more," Eileen said, blowing an arrow of smoke and passing the joint.

Luce inhaled and held it for the beat of three. "Pretty much," she said. "I've never been any good at confrontation."

"Hey!" Eileen had poked her in the arm, hard.

"Hey what?" Eileen laughed and hit her harder.

"Why are you hitting me?" Luce asked, and stood up. Eileen

followed, took the joint, drew in a long drag, considered her, and slapped Luce's face with her left hand. Bongo was wide awake and concerned, but he too seemed confused about what he should do.

"Wrong response." Another slap. Harder, enough to sting. Luce turned to walk away, but Eileen seized her by the shoulders and shook her. "C'mon, what should you say when someone hauls off and smacks you?" *Or stabs you?*

"Stop hitting me," Luce said after Eileen gave her another gentler slap and handed her back the joint.

"You win a prize," Eileen whispered. She pulled Luce to her. The kiss moved from gentle to urgent, to an entwining of tongues and muffled moans. By the end they were back on the grass, Luce sprawled on top of Eileen.

"Good prize," Luce said. "And I get it. Dumb Philosophy 101, but I get it. It may even make a little sense."

The rising moon shone through the glass, casting a blue-green glow on the room and over the sleeping loft where the two naked women lay sweaty and entwined. Eileen had kept her word, and Luce had screamed her name so loudly that the pastured cattle had probably heard. Bongo certainly had, and barked to be let in the house. Eileen had teeth marks on her shoulder and scratches on her freckled back. Both of their faces were wet with one another's juices. They kissed, rested, arose, and showered together, and began again—with moderation to the previous desperate urgency.

Even by the inadequate light of the moon and two candles Luce could see that Eileen's scars now stood out as scarlet lines against her pale skin. Her own flesh was dark from the outdoors and sunbathing. Janice hated tan lines. *How could she love someone that shallow? Still love her?*

"You are going to have to go back." Eileen was the first to recover. "I know that. You have bits of her all through you."

"I don't want to."

"But you will."

"Yes." *But only because I met you and now I would be ashamed to admit lacking the courage to do it. Demand love on my terms.* Luce drew a finger down Eileen's arm, shoulder to fingertips.

"What happened to him?" Luce asked, staring up at the slanting ceiling. "You're here. You survived, so..."

"I took the knife away and I killed him. I'm not the tiniest bit sorry about it," Eileen said. "I made the decision that I wanted to live." Her voice was even and inflectionless; all of the warmth had gone out of it. After a while they slept.

"I wish I could stay here," Luce said, swallowing a spoonful of buttered oatmeal. Through the windows she could see Eleanor Roosevelt in the crystalline early morning light, standing by the paddock fence, staring toward the house.

"I wish you could too," Eileen said. "But I'm not your honey bun, sugar plum right now, though I kinda wish I was. However things work out I want you to come back. Bring her with you. Maybe I can help straighten her out."

"I'll bring her—if things go that way," Luce said. "But I think I'll have to be the one to do the straightening. Otherwise I might be back without her."

"You'd be welcome," Eileen said.

And the last kiss was the best yet.

As Eileen had told her, there wasn't any cell phone reception until she got within a couple of miles of Mazurton. There she pulled over to the side of the road and punched in the familiar number. Janice answered and they talked. And cried. Afterward Luce carefully turned the truck and trailer around, and she and Bongo and Eleanor Roosevelt headed back north. Toward Wyoming.

CULLY'S RUN

Cheyenne Blue

Αpril 2007 - Bogong High Plains, Victoria, Australia

"You shouldn't be here!"

She was beak-nosed and quivering, lean and tight-strung as fencing wire. Underneath her fleece beanie, her eyes were fierce.

"No?" Lou continued squatting at the small fire, enamel mug of coffee in her hand. "Who says?" By her side, Kelsey growled a stern warning.

The woman stalked a farther pace into the clearing amid the snowgums. "The National Park Service. The Mountain Cattlemen's Association. The Victorian State Government."

"The government!" Lou hooted. "Don't see no stuffed politicians here."

Swinging her small pack from her shoulders, the woman leveled a glare at Lou. "And I say it!"

Eyes crinkling in amusement, Lou took another draught of coffee. The liquid steamed in the crisp air. "Now I'm really worried. You and whose army is going to move me on?"

"Listen," the woman hissed. "You know bloody well this is the Alpine National Park. And cattle have been banned for the last two years. You must take your horse, put out your fire, and drive your herd out the way you came in."

"Herd? You're too kind." Lou glanced over to where Daisy and her calf grazed placidly. "And, I'll be another three days if I go out the way I came in. If I keep going, I'll be in Dargo tomorrow."

"You're destroying the ecosystem. Their hooves cause erosion; they encourage imbalance with their selective eating. And they're banned! As they should be." She jammed her hands on her hips and glared. The setting sun lit her curly hair to a golden corona, silhouetting her wiry figure, swathed in Gore-Tex and fleece.

Not pretty, thought Lou, idly, but interesting. But right now, a whinging greenie that was rattling her peace.

"You're disturbing my ecosystem," she said pointedly. "I was quite happy, bothering no one, until you came along. Shouldn't you get back to your pretty marked path before dark? Wouldn't want you bushed on the high plains. Rescue attempts are a pain in the arse, not to mention a waste of public funds."

"I left the trail because I saw your marks. Hoofprints and cattle tracks. And a dog. The last two of which are banned in—"

"National Parks. Yes, I know. I heard you the first time." She unfurled, rising to her feet in one smooth movement. "I've had enough of you. I suggest you fuck off back to your renovated Victorian terrace in some poncey Melbourne suburb and renew your subscription to *G Magazine*. Then I suggest you meet your equally annoying friends—no doubt a bunch of overpaid lawyers and marketing gurus who bond over lattes and congrat-ulate each other for being strong independent women—and you can relate how I single-handedly destroyed the whole high plains ecosystem, before you write a letter to *The Age* about state-funded child care and the quality of organic custard apples in the Prahran Market, and forget about me. And believe me, it can't happen soon enough as far as I'm concerned."

Lou turned her back and stalked over to where Ruby grazed placidly. Running her hand down the bay's shoulder, she took steady deep breaths. Her gaze passed over Ruby's neck and centered on the snowgums edging the clearing, their mottled bark and clean-edged limbs silver in the gloaming. She took a lungful of crisp mountain air and focused on the boulders and tufts of hummocky grass.

"Look, I'm sorry."

Christ, that woman moved quieter than a tiger snake.

"I didn't mean to be so confrontational."

"You've got 'confrontational' down to an art form." Lou stayed with her hands on her horse's neck, feeling the shift of muscle underneath the burgeoning winter coat.

"It's just that this area is different. Special. Australia's got so little snow country that it needs to be preserved."

"Preserved. Pickled like an onion. Made into an exhibit to be admired. No." Lou turned and faced the other woman. "That's where you're wrong. This is living, breathing landscape, not a museum piece. And that's where I come in. I'm not merely borrowing this land to walk upon it over Melbourne Cup weekend; I'm part of it, my history is here, in the high country. The mountain creeks run through my dreams. My horse's hooves tread the dirt, and yes, my cattle roam the high plains. Or they did, until your lot interfered."

"Your family are mountain cattlemen?"

Lou nodded and her blunt fingernails dug deeper into Ruby's mane.

"We've held Cully's Run since 1860, when my great, great, great grandfather came over from Ireland and took over the run. He got a few cattle here and there—rustled some, if the tales are true—until he had a decent mob. And every spring, he'd drove them up Insolvency Spur, just him and his brother who was soft in the head, and their dogs. He lost a few over the side of the trail, and he lost his brother when the ground went from under his horse and he was thrown down a cliff. But he kept going, and he built his run up. My family still holds it.

"And until the stickybeaks got involved, we kept that life. At the start of summer, we drove our cattle up through Dargo to the high plains and let them roam, growing sleek and fat, and every autumn we'd muster them up, take them back down to lower pasture. And in the meantime, we'd check on them, mend fences, maintain the timber huts that the bushwalkers now use and the hoons burn down most summers. We'd mend tanks, dig culverts, fix washouts in the roads—the roads that now carry city people in their four-wheel drives up for a weekend of adventure. We know this land, better than you can ever imagine. Don't you try to tell me about this place. It's my land."

The other woman was silent. In the half-light her thin face was thoughtful. "So why are you here now?"

"I can't give it up. The government has banned the cattlemen from the plains; so what! I'm not going to be ordered around by some drongo in a suit. So every spring and autumn, I drive a couple of cattle up the old pathways. I don't let them roam free; I just take them along the old tracks from Dargo up to the high plains and back again. We're not harming anyone, and you're not going to stop me. So, now that you've made your point and I've listened, I suggest you turn on your GPS unit and get your pretty butt back on the trail and down to your

camp. The light's going and I'd hate to have to call out Bush
Search and Rescue."

"I'm not camping. I've booked a room at the Dargo pub."

"You're kidding, right? You'll never find your way in the
dark. I suggest you git on down the track as far as you can and
make camp before it's completely dark."

"Didn't you listen? I said, I'm not camping. Look." She
rummaged through the small pack, bringing out muesli bars,
fruit, bottles of water and energy drink, gloves, and an extra
fleece. "No tent. No sleeping bag."

"So what are you going to do? Dig out your satellite phone
to call for rescue and dob me in at the same time?"

The other woman advanced. Close up, she was smaller,
scrawny even. Her brown hair curled over her shoulders,
contained by the fleece beanie. Her eyes were blue, and her
skin had a weather-beaten look, prematurely aged by the harsh
Aussie sun.

"Cattlemen's code."

"What?"

"Don't you people have a code, whereby you help each other
out? Not just cattlemen; no one leaves anyone else stuck in the
bush. I'll stop here with you tonight. May I share your tent?"

"What tent? I don't see any tent, do you, Kelsey?" Lou
addressed the dog. "Me and Kel here, we share my swag." With
a wave of her hand, she indicated the canvas sausage on the far
side of the small fire. The self-contained bedroll was sturdy, with
a waterproof cover and merely a hood to keep the rain off the
occupant. While it was roomy for one, two would be more than
cozy.

"Oh."

Lou studied her lazily while she deliberated. Really, it would
be no hardship to share her swag with this woman. She had a

surprisingly wide, sensual mouth, and compressed energy—the sort that often indicated an enthusiastic bed partner. Lou could imagine her sinewy legs tangled with her own, could imagine her coffee-breath kiss.

The other woman swung back and stuck out a hand. "If we're sharing a swag, at least we should know each other's name. I'm Derrie."

"Lou."

Derrie's grip was firm and sure. "Thanks."

"No worries. Just try and keep your mouth shut." Lou walked back to the small fire and picked up her cold coffee, throwing dregs onto the ground. "Want a coffee? It's instant, not a skinny mochachino soy milk latte or whatever the hell you normally drink, but it's hot."

"You're the one who told me to keep my mouth shut." Derrie picked up the blackened billy lying by the fire and filled it from the waterskin. "Why don't you keep your own obnoxious opinions to yourself? You don't know me at all, but you're judging me by how you perceive I like my coffee."

Lou stared into the fire, watching the eucalyptus wood, heart-red and glowing. It cracked, the oil within exploding like a whip-crack in the evening. "You're right; you didn't deserve that."

"I'm not blameless." Derrie smiled, and her angular face gained an appeal, the warmth suddenly apparent. "Shall we call a truce?"

The billy boiled over in an explosion of steam. Lou picked it off the fire with a forked stick. "Truce. Over coffee. Hope you like it unsweetened and black."

"I do."

"Lucky for you!" She held out the mug. "Only got the one. We'll have to share. Pull up a log and sit."

For a few minutes they were silent, passing the mug back and forth between them. Lou fancied it was warm from more than the coffee. The darkness fell like a blanket in the abrupt way it did on the high plains. The cockatoos wheeled back to roost, and a kookaburra cackled maniacally and then fell silent. Lou threw a handful of gum leaves onto the fire, watching as they flared into flame, their fresh scent filling the air. Standing, she went to check on Ruby hobbled nearby, and to make sure that she could see the dim shapes of Daisy and her calf in the darkness. Kelsey pattered at her heels. Away from the fire, the air was sharp and clean. She stood, listening to the night sounds of the bush: The squawk of a bird; the rhythmic thump of a 'roo disturbed by her scent. The snuffle and blunder of something solid in the undergrowth, a wombat maybe.

Returning to the fire, she stood in the shadows outside the glow watching her uninvited guest. Derrie hunkered on a log, cradling the coffee, her face thoughtful as she stared into the fire. No, not attractive, not her usual sort of woman, but she had a raw appeal, an energy, a leashed passion. And they would share her swag. Lou's stomach fluttered gently in anticipation. "You might have to sleep outside tonight, Kel," she murmured. "No room for three."

Back at the fire, she busied herself with the cooking. She turned the spuds in the ashes, and heaped more coals on the top of the Dutch oven already buried in the embers.

"I can contribute some energy bars and chocolate," Derrie said.

"Chocolate could be good. Lucky I have enough food here. I did an extra spud as Kel likes them."

"Poor Kel will miss out." Derrie ruffled the dog's fur.

They ate in silence, sharing the same enamel dish and fork, their backs against a log as they took it in turns to scoop up the beef stew. When the leftovers had cooled, Lou gave them to Kel, wiping the billy and plates with a handful of grass.

Accepting a piece of chocolate from Derrie, she tilted her face upwards. The swath of stars burned bright in the indigo sky, a ribbon of light grazing the tops of the snowgums, lighting the clearing with its cold glow. The Southern Cross hung low in the sky.

Derrie stirred, rising from her log and stretching. "I'm turning in."

Lou nodded, unwilling to leave the brilliant night, even for the promise of a warm body aligned with hers. Instead, she stretched out on her back, arms over her head. The coldness of the ground seeped into her body, but she didn't move. Underneath the sky, her favorite time. Overhead, the sky blazed with the weight of the stars. So many stars, so many million pulsating points of light. Lou lay dreaming, gazing through half-closed eyes, until it felt as if the Earth fell away, leaving her suspended in the glowing universe.

It was an hour before she rose and paced over to where the swag humped down on the far side of the fire. She tamped down the fire, made a last check on Ruby, and sent Kel out around the cattle. Kel would alert her if anything was amiss. Shucking her clothes, she rolled them into a ball, and leaving her boots under the hood, she stooped and listened. Derrie's breathing was slow and steady, but Lou sensed she wasn't asleep—her breathing was too careful, too even. There was a tension in the air, an anticipation. What was Derrie wearing in bed? With a thrum of anticipation, she pushed the rolled-up clothes down in the swag, so that they'd be warm and dry for the morning. Carefully, she slid in alongside Derrie. It wasn't easy; the bedroll was narrow, designed for one, and her feet and legs brushed warm flesh.

Derrie was lying on her back. Lou turned on her side, facing the other woman. Kel pattered back, sliding under the swag's hood, her panting breath on Lou's face as she tried to slide in.

"Outside, Kel," Lou said, in a low voice.

With a sigh, the blue heeler settled, nose to tail.

Lou propped her head on her hand, studying Derrie. Her features were softened by pools of shadow, her hawk nose and angular cheeks smoothed by the overlay of starlight. Her eyes were open. Lou hesitated; she knew what she wanted, sensed it wouldn't be unwelcome—two strangers thrown into proximity. What more natural than they share their bodies along with the swag? But she didn't want it to be an obligation, rent for the night's accommodation.

Her hand moved over, seeking Derrie, coming to rest on her flat stomach. No T-shirt. That was a good start, but her muscles were drum tight and quivering. Lou slid her hand down, around to Derrie's hip. A thin band of elastic interrupted the flow of fingers over skin. She touched it, slipping beneath, feeling thin skin over sharp bone.

"What are you doing?" Derrie's voice cracked into the night like a whip.

Lou went for broke. "Seducing you."

Derrie huffed a laugh. "I could just give you fifty bucks for the space if you want payment, although the tourist bureau might have something to say about the standard."

"It's not payment," Lou said, carefully feeling her way, even as her fingers dared another inch of skin. "I thought it might be welcomed." The coil of anticipation in her belly wound a little tighter.

Derrie turned her head and her eyes glittered. "All we do is fight."

"Then fight me." Lou held her breath; if she'd been reading this wrong...

With a lunge, Derrie ducked her head, pressing her lips to the crease of Lou's neck and shoulder. Small, sharp teeth nipped her skin, and her breath burned Lou's collarbone. Her hand—surprisingly strong—pressed Lou backwards into the side of the swag.

Lou's breath left her in a rush, and Kel growled a warning.

"It's okay, Kel," she managed, before her mouth was covered by Derrie's, all hot breath and tongue, all moisture and searching lips. Derrie's hands roamed freely, down from her collarbone, down over the slope of breast, to find a nipple. It peaked sharply against Derrie's fingers.

Derrie rolled and pinched, and the delicious edge of pain sent shafts of delight down deep into Lou's belly. Derrie's mouth suckled hard on her neck, and the bloom of pain spread warmly over her skin. The other woman had the upper hand, and Lou let her take full advantage, moving unresistingly onto her back when Derrie moved further on top. Lean, sinewy legs tangled with Lou's, and she thrilled at the friction of skin on skin; Derrie's thigh moving insistently between her own, her warm flesh pressing on her core.

Lou wrapped one hand into the thick hair that tickled her neck and tugged, forcing Derrie's face up. She was flushed, her mouth open as she panted in the close confines of the swag. With a growl, Lou pulled her face down to her own, and they kissed again, tongues tangling and echoing the thrust and fierceness of their bodies. Lou traced the bumps of Derrie's spine, curving her hand lower, over flat boyish buttocks, as firm and muscular as Ruby's rump. Her slight breasts were mashed into Lou's own fuller ones, her nipples as hard and round as cherry pits.

Now that the invitation was offered and accepted, the urgency muted, sliding seamlessly into a lazy passion. Lou's

world contracted to a dark and secret place of animalistic
noises and movement. The swag's hood blocked much of the
starlight, leaving the two of them encased in dim shadows and
confining cloth. The rustle of the inner sheet sounded harsh and
loud, amplified by their closed quarters; and Derrie's breathing,
fast and rasping, drowned out the drumbeat of Lou's heart. It
was elemental: touch, sound, and smell. Derrie was musky, her
hair smoky from the campfire, the sharp tang of eucalyptus, the
warm fug of a body that works itself hard.

For long minutes Lou explored, finding the way around
Derrie's body, mapping how her palms curved over planes
of muscle and flesh, tracing the edge of a breast, the arch of
buttock, the wing of hip, and reaching down to find steely
muscles and firm, toned thighs. In turn, Derrie's fingers walked
their way around Lou's flesh, circling slowly, teasingly, never
quite contacting where Lou wanted them the most.

Derrie shifted again, so that the two women lay facing
each other. Enough starlight filtered through that Lou could
see Derrie's eyes, open and glittering, intent upon her face.
Now, she could explore properly. Her fingers sought the other
woman's slight breast, tracing the swell, walking in decreasing
circles toward her nipple. When she finally reached her goal, her
lips followed her fingers, and she shuffled forward, taking the
nubbin between her lips, suckling, feeling Derrie's shaky sigh in
the hitch of her breathing. Gently, she bit, thrilling at the instinc-
tive arch of Derrie's body toward hers.

Derrie wasn't passive. Her hand tangled in Lou's hair, pulling
her up until they could kiss again. Unlike the urgency of their
first kiss, this was a dreamy languorous thing, a feather-light
touch of heat and starlight. Touch and withdraw, their lips met,
tasted, and parted again. Derrie's hand snaked down between
their bodies, along the edge of Lou's thigh, reversing direction

and creeping up the inner surface. Caught in the confines of the swag, Lou tried to raise her upper leg, allow the smaller woman better access, but the sheet didn't give, and the best she managed was a small space.

It was enough. Derrie's fingers moved up, moved in, touching hair, stroking her slick folds, and sliding slowly between. One finger, two. Derrie's fingers twisted, pistoning, her thumb rubbing insistently on Lou's clit.

"I wish I could taste you," Derrie murmured into her mouth. "I wish I could push my mouth against your cunt and lick you until you came."

"Oh, yes," breathed Lou, "do it, please."

"No room," said Derrie, succinctly, and her fingers insinuated themselves farther into the slick channel.

In between the coils of feeling, the spiraling pressure in her belly, Lou could appreciate the skillful fingers. Derrie was intent on discovery, and Lou gave herself over to the sensations. Her hands clenched on Derrie's hips as she ground onto her fingers, letting the pressure build until she overflowed in an explosion of climax, as fast and fierce and gushing as a mountain creek.

Derrie pulled her fingers from Lou's cunt, bringing them up to her lips. "Sweet," she murmured, as she licked them clean.

As her heartbeat returned to normal, Lou wrapped her arms around the other woman, aligning their bodies tightly. Dipping her head, she explored the curve of neck and shoulder, letting her lips drift over her skin. It was warm in the confines of the swag, and she tasted salt, smelled the grassy tang of fresh sweat.

"Turn around," she murmured, pushing on Derrie's hip until she complied.

Derrie's buttocks pushed backwards into her thighs, and Lou raised her own so that they were spooned tightly together. Now she had the entire sweet package to explore at her leisure.

Her hands glided smoothly from shoulder, around and over her breasts, down to the thick patch of hair between her thighs.

Derrie shuddered in her arms. "Get on with it," she said, tightly.

"Impatient." A smile curved her mouth, and she nuzzled aside the wiry hair and rested her lips on the nape of Derrie's neck. Deliberately, she combed through the hair between her lover's thighs, parting the coarse curls, tickling lightly on her pussy lips.

Derrie's buttocks pushed insistently back once more, her body coiled and tight against Lou's own.

Taking pity, Lou cupped her mound, pushing her fingers firmly into the thicket, parting her folds to delve between. Derrie's clit was a rigid pearl, slick and hot. Lou circled lightly, not knowing how heavy a touch the other woman liked.

Derrie's hand jerked down, pressing over Lou's, forcing a firmer feel. Emboldened, Lou rubbed harder, spreading her creamy moisture around, until Derrie stiffened, her heels drumming into Lou's calves with an urgent, staccato beat. Her sigh was loud in the musky darkness, a long susurration of completion. Gently, she lifted Lou's hand from her cunt, cupping it with her own, holding it against her breast.

Lou curled up again around her lover, and settled in for sleep.

October 2007 - Bogong High Plains, Victoria, Australia

"You shouldn't be here!"

She was beak-nosed and quivering; lean and tight-strung as fencing wire. Underneath her fleece beanie, her eyes beamed in pleasure.

"No?" Lou continued squatting at the small fire, enamel mug

of coffee in her hand. "You came back." By her side, Kelsey yapped a small welcome.

Derrie slung her hefty pack down by the fire. "I did. But this time, I've got camping gear, so if I'm imposing, you can tell me where to go."

"No," said Lou. "You're not imposing."

Overhead the cockatoos wheeled like fluttering rags against the charcoal sky, and although the air was heavy with impending rain, the evening stretched warmly in front of her.

BAREBACK

DeJay

I push through the screen door onto the porch, leaving Maggie to deal with the dishes while I come out to get some air and enjoy a cold drink. For a moment I stand still, leaning on the rail, then stretch from left to right and back again. My back is stiff and achy, my knee swollen from too much use. I've been riding the fenceline all day making repairs with my foreman, digging postholes and hanging barbed wire, both of which did little to ease my arthritic body.

I relax and listen to the quiet of the evening, thankful to be erect instead of still in the saddle. I'm always amazed at how noisy the quiet can be if you know what your ears capture. I can hear the water as it ripples over the rocks in the brook out back. The chickadees call to their mates, while an owl to the west is on the hunt for its evening meal. A slight breeze rustles the leaves on the mammoth oak tree here in the front of the house.

I lean a hip on the rail and pick up my beer from the floor, and after a long pull on the bottle I shift my shoulders and rotate

my neck, the tension of a hard day on the range slowly evapo-
rating. I shake my head, disgusted with the aches and pains.
When the hell did I get so old?

I decide to walk down to the paddock and check on two
brood mares, both about to foal. I can hear Moon neighing as I
approach. The horse greets me with ears up and nickers, moving
slowly to the fence, where I greet her with a thorough rub of her
muzzle. "How you doing, girl?" I run my hand down her neck
and pat her. "Sounds like tonight could be the night, whadda ya
think, hmm?"

"Who are you talking to?"

A smile sweeps across my lips. "It's about damn time,
woman." Though I can't really see clearly in the dark, Maggie's
image is emblazoned on my mind, her sweet smile, sun-kissed
cheeks, and strands of auburn hair mixed mostly with gray now.
Her loose braid hangs down the middle of her back. Tight curls
break away to frame her heart-shaped face.

She touches my shoulder before turning to talk with Moon.
I watch as she whispers to the horse, a secret language that only
they seem to understand. Moon's head bobs up and down as
though in agreement.

I walk up behind Maggie, wrap my arms around her middle,
nuzzle her neck, and kiss her cheek. "So what's the verdict?"

She leans back against me, radiating warmth. "She's going to
foal tonight, I'm sure of it."

"I agree. We should take her into the birthing stall where she'll
be more comfortable. Will you get the door to the stables?"

I release Maggie and enter the paddock, moving slowly so
Moon doesn't get spooked. "It's okay, girl, I'm just going to
check you out." I reach up and grasp her mane with one hand
to hold her while I run my other over her swollen belly. She
flinches slightly. I move to her rump and examine the tailhead

muscles. They're soft and lax, a good indication that Moon's time is near.

Maggie has returned, and hands me a halter.

"What do you think?"

When I give the lead rope a gentle tug, Moon walks quietly along beside me. I guide her into the stall and then rub her down again. "Her water hasn't broken yet, so it will be a while, but she'll be happier in here." I bring her fresh water, step out of the stall, and close the gate.

"How long?"

I grin at my impatient wife. "Do I look like Mother Nature?"

She swats at my arm. "Take a guess, damn it."

"Definitely tonight, maybe a couple hours, I'm not really sure." The worry is clear on Maggie's face. "She's going to do fine. I'll stay out here tonight with her just in case."

Maggie hugs me tightly. "I love you."

"Love you too." I lean in and kiss her gently. "Maybe later, after the new foal arrives, we can celebrate?" I waggle my eyebrows lecherously at her.

Maggie shakes her head. "Let's just see if you're still awake later, old woman." She moves to push away.

I kiss her again, cup her ass, pull her closer still. "We have a date when this is over, don't forget that."

Maggie cups my face, presses her lips to mine in gentle surrender. "I'll be back."

"Why?"

She releases me and walks away, her jeans hugging her round hips. Tantalizing hips that sway with each step. "I'm going to get us some jackets and a blanket. If you're real good, I might bring some coffee."

I call after her. "You don't have to stay with me."

"I'm not." I hear her snort. "I'm staying with Moon." Her

laughter echoes as she strolls up to the main house.

I reach up and rub Moon's muzzle. "Hear that? She loves you more." The horse stares at me as if she agrees. Her ears prick up, and she nickers deep in her throat. "Don't be afraid, you're gonna do just fine, and I'll be here the whole time." I pat her neck, step back, walk to the wall, and flip the switch to dim the lights. That will help to settle her. I go into the stable's office on the far wall, where I gather towels, rubber gloves, and surgical scrub. Once Moon's water breaks, there won't be time. I want to be sure we're prepared. I grab the phone from the office and plug it into the jack by Moon's stall, just in case.

Maggie returns almost an hour later with coats, blankets, and a picnic basket.

"What took you so long?"

She glares at me as if I'm a spoiled child. "I made you brownies, if you must know." Maggie glances at Moon and back to me. "How's she doing?"

I start to laugh. "You're like a nervous Nellie. Relax, this is going to take as long as it takes. You can't rush her or upset her."

She sticks her tongue out at me. We've been anxious for weeks now. This is Moon's first time, but with luck she'll produce a healthy offspring. Who knows, maybe even a champion.

My nose alerts me to the scent of fresh brewed coffee and the heavenly aroma of the brownies. "Smells great!" I reach for the basket.

She pulls it out of my reach. "What can I do?"

I walk to the stall across from Moon's and motion Maggie inside. I've set up a small table and some bales of hay to lie on while we await this much-anticipated event. I have a small electric lantern lit as well, so we can see while we wait. "Relax, honey, this could take a while."

"Do you have the towels, the kits, and...?"

I gently nudge her into the stall and relieve her of one of the blankets. "Yes, I do, and everything is ready." I shake out the cover and spread it over the top of the hay bales.

Maggie places the basket on the table and opens it, pulling out a thermos and two cups. "Coffee?"

"Please." I slip the jacket on to ward off the chill of night and then attempt to sneak a peak at the brownies, a personal favorite.

Maggie's hand slaps mine away. "I'll get you one, but you can only have three, so pace yourself." With that she pulls out a paper plate with a small one-inch square of brownie.

"Why?"

"Your blood pressure is why, and you know it." She hands me the plate and closes the lid.

"You weren't worried about my blood pressure the other night on the porch or this morning." My temper makes my voice harsher than I mean it to be.

Maggie takes my hand. "I always worry, but you hate that I do."

I shrug. "Sorry."

She leans in and kisses my cheek.

"Do we have whipped cream?"

Maggie picks up her coffee and takes a sip. "Didn't you use all of that the other morning?" Her voice holds a hint of admonishment.

"Oh, yeah." The memory of her breasts covered in fluffy whipped cream makes me smile. "What about chocolate syrup?"

She shakes her finger at me. "You used that Saturday night." The rasp of her voice lets me know she's still not forgiven me.

"Oops."

"Yeah, I'll oops you. I'm still trying to get the stain out. Those were our good silk sheets, too." Maggie pinches the last piece of brownie from my plate and pops it in her mouth. "Carol wanted to know if we had been mud wrestling."

I want to laugh but know better. Instead I put down the empty plate and my coffee, pull her close, and capture her lips in a kiss. The heat simmering just beneath the surface is the way it's always been with us.

Maggie tugs my hair, hard. "Stop." She walks over to Moon's stall, and I follow her.

Moon sees Maggie and comes to the gate, bobbing her head. Maggie pets the horse, the love between them a wonder to experience.

I wrap my arms around Maggie and nuzzle her neck. "Excited?"

She nods, tears in her eyes.

I push her hair out of the way in order to trail some kisses across the back of her neck.

Maggie arches her neck to give me better access. "Did you get the fence repaired out in the north pasture?"

"Yes, ma'am." I slip my hands up to cup her breasts, her nipples hard little nubs under the material. "Matt and I dug all new postholes and set them in along the entire breach." I run my tongue along her jaw. "The wood was rotted. I think some deer or elk took it down. Nothing malicious." I reach for the button on her plaid shirt.

She stops my progress. "I told you the last time, no more outdoor activities."

I move my hands down to her hips and pull her tight. Her ass covers my crotch, and my hips jerk in anticipation.

"Bet."

"Hmm?" I keep applying soft kisses as I move my hands back to her breasts.

"Bernice Elizabeth Thatcher." She gasps as I increase the pressure on her nipples. "Ohh, please...honey."

I release her breasts and hold her close, burying my face in her hair, taking in the smell of her. A mixture of baking brownies, apple spice from her shampoo, and perspiration after a long day of chores. "You know, there was a time when you wouldn't have asked me to stop."

Maggie turns in my arms. "Yes, and we were a lot younger and more able-bodied."

"My body's still able, it's just slower now." I kiss her on the lips, and whisper in her ear, "I thought you liked slower." Maggie turns back to the horse, a blush coloring her cheeks.

I stand behind her, content for the moment. "We could always use the accommodations across the aisle; I might even come up with a surprise for you."

Maggie looks at me for what seems like minutes, a smile spreading across her face. "I fell for that when we were younger. I'm not that naïve any longer."

When I tug her hand and step backward, she holds her ground, uncertainty in her eyes.

"Trust me."

"Yeah, right. Last time I trusted you, we almost got caught butt naked in the truck up by the lake, remember?"

Before I can answer I hear Moon neigh loudly. The horse is lying in the hay, amniotic fluid rushing from her body. Maggie and I turn in time to see the white sac begin to protrude from the horse's vulva. "What should we do?" Maggie's hands are on the gate, her entire body tense.

"We just stand here and talk softly. So far it looks like she knows what she's doing." I put my arm about Maggie's shoulder, trying to settle her down.

"Should we call Eric?"

"Not yet, we'll know if she gets in trouble, and he's only ten minutes from here." I rub my hand up and down her arm for comfort. "By the way, we *didn't* get caught naked and that's all that's important."

She shakes her head. "No thanks to you."

"Details." I walk back across the aisle and get my coffee cup.

"What about the time before that, at the picnic in town? Behind the snow-cone stand? I know you didn't forget that."

Moon's contractions are beginning in earnest. She moans to let us know she's not happy. So far though, she's not in distress, either. "It should be quick now." I place one hand at the small of Maggie's back and take a sip of coffee from the cup in my other hand. "As for the incident at the town picnic, that *was* a small miscalculation on my part." The memory makes me smile.

Maggie's eyes are on Moon. The mare's head jerks, her nostrils flare, her eyes widen as a shudder goes through her. Now we can see the foal's legs extending from the birth canal. "Is she…"

"She's fine, so far everything is normal." I kiss Maggie's cheek and give her a squeeze. "Relax, talk to me."

Maggie looks at me and then back at Moon. Her hand covers her mouth, trembling.

"She's okay, I promise you. We've done this before, remember."

"She's my baby." Maggie grips the rail, her knuckles white. For every contraction Moon feels, Maggie's breath hitches a bit more.

"Talk to me."

"What about?"

"Anything."

She stands there staring at her horse, her pride and joy. Moments pass, and then suddenly, "What about the time at the drive-in, way back when there *were* still drive-ins?"

I stop for a minute as the memory washes over me. We were in the back seat of my Ford Galaxy, and I already had her shirt off. I had just pulled down her shorts and spread her wide when there was a tap on the window. "Now that was fun." I leer at her, knowing she remembers where we finished our activities that night.

"Why can't you learn we do not do well in the outdoors?" Maggie's eyes never leave the mare. Pressure from lying down has broken the white sac now; the fluid will lubricate the birth canal and the foal. She rolls over on her side and begins the process of pushing with each contraction. Things are progressing well.

I don't take my eyes off the mare. "It's going to be soon."

Maggie is smiling, tears in her eyes. She turns to me, excitement written on her face. "Do you remember when my father caught us here in the barn?" Her smile turns nostalgic. "There would have been a shotgun wedding if it had been legal."

The memory floods back, and a small shudder goes through me. "Well, yeah, we were both naked, and I had three fingers buried deep inside you. When your orgasm hit, you screamed loud enough for people to hear you three counties over." An image of Mr. Reilly's face floods my mind. "We only got caught because you have a big mouth." I lean in and kiss her on the lips. "But I do like making you scream."

Maggie turns the cutest shade of red. Before I can comment, a groan erupts from Moon; now the nose and head of the foal are visible. "You're doing good girl, keep going, you're gonna make us proud." I can see tears running down Maggie's cheeks.

"I was afraid Daddy was going to have a heart attack. Remember he came running into the barn, his rifle in hand." She wraps her arms across her middle. "I thought he might actually shoot you."

I nod and grasp her hand, trying to steady her fears. "He took it pretty well considering the times."

"Remember how he dragged us into the house?" Maggie squeezes my hand.

"Oh, yeah. He had us march ahead of him, with the gun aimed at my back." The hair on my neck stands at the memory.

Moon lets loose with a cry as another contraction surges through her. We watch in awe as she pushes and the neck and shoulders of the foal burst through the vulva. Moon raises her head. "I think the next contraction will do it."

Maggie watches Moon, captivated. "Remember when we got to his study, he had us sit. He poured a drink before he turned back to us." Again tears run down Maggie's face; I'm not sure if they're for the horse or the memory of her beloved father.

"I remember, honey."

She smiles at me. "He wanted to know what your intentions were. I have never seen you so scared."

I bristle at the comment, but know it to be true. "Hell yes, I was scared. The gun was lying on the desk."

Maggie squeezes my hand. I wince at the pain. "Easy there, tiger, I'm not made of stone."

She wraps her arms around me and pulls me close. "You were also brave and stood right up to him. I was so proud of you."

I wrap my arm around her shoulder and rest my head against hers. "We had discussed it. You knew I wanted to be with you, I loved you. It was time to tell him no matter what the consequences. I didn't want to hide anymore."

Moon groans, and pushes once again with another contraction ripping through her. As if by magic the foal slides completely free from the mare and lands softly in the fresh hay.

Maggie turns to me and buries her face in my chest. I can feel her soft sobs within the cradle of my arms. "It's okay, the worst is over."

Both mare and foal lie there in the hay, relaxing after the ordeal of birth. Blood still pumps between them via the umbilical cord.

Maggie kisses my cheek. "Thank you."

I'm surprised by the gesture. "For what?"

"For staying with Moon, for talking to me." She runs her hand along my cheek and cups my jaw. "For making me remember, for loving me."

I lower my head, and my lips graze hers. "I do love you, always have."

Moments later, Moon neighs loudly, rocks, and stands. A shudder goes through her body before she moves to her offspring, the cord breaking in the process. Moon's pain is not yet over, with contractions to expel the afterbirth still to come, but she knows what is required. She begins calmly cleaning the foal, nudging it to stand. The bonding process begins.

After a few minutes I go in briefly to help out with a towel, though Moon is doing fine on her own. "It's a filly!"

Maggie lifts her head and turns to the scene before us. "She's beautiful, look at her."

"Yes, she is."

"Do you think she'll remain black?" Maggie leans against the gate, stretching to get a better view of our newest property. "Oh, look, she's got one white sock, just like Dante's." The awe in Maggie's voice makes me smile.

I squeeze her shoulders and laugh. Maggie and I will be together twenty-five years next month. My love has grown stronger over time, and she grows more beautiful with each passing day.

I release Maggie and leave her to watch her charges while

I get the wheelbarrow and rake. Shortly I will be able to clean up the dirty hay and spread clean for dam and foal to rest in. As I return to the stall I see Moon's filly is standing on wobbly legs. Maggie and I watch in wonder for long moments until the foal reaches under the mare and begins to nurse. Now that she is nursing, the afterbirth will be expelled easier. Mother Nature provides, and the new mother and filly will do just fine. A sense of calm settles over both of us as we take in the scene. No matter how many times I witness a birth I am still in awe. "Amazing."

Maggie grasps my hand. "That it is, Bet, that it is." She uses her other hand to wipe her brow.

"You can go in the house now. I'll finish up here." I tug Maggie to get her attention. "A nice hot shower might relax you, help with the stiffness of standing for so long." She has a bruised hip, a reminder from falling off a horse a couple of years ago.

She shakes her head. "No. I want to watch her for a while. You can go in if you're tired."

"I'm staying. There's still work to be done." I turn to pull the wheelbarrow up to the gate. "I'm happy for your company."

A short time later as Maggie and I stand sipping our third— or is it fourth?—cup of coffee, Moon expels the afterbirth. She moves over to the side of the stall, the foal following on her gangly legs. I slip in and begin the process of raking up the bloody, wet hay.

Maggie fills a bucket with oats and hangs it for Moon, who needs to rebuild her strength now. She fills the trough with fresh water and rubs Moon's muzzle. "You did amazing today. Thank you, sweetie." Maggie hugs the horse's neck.

As I distribute the last of the clean hay in the stall, I turn to her. "I think you love that horse more than you love me."

She turns and smiles mischievously. "It's close, but I'm pretty sure you come in first."

I roll the wheelbarrow outside, dropping the rake on the way, and then move up behind Maggie and pull her into my arms. "Good thing, woman, 'cause I get jealous real easy."

She pushes against me. "What if someone comes in here?"

"There's no one around. Eric is home; he left before dinner. The crew went into town." I waggle my eyebrows and leer at her. "We're all alone."

Maggie turns in my arms and grasps my shoulders. "I don't know who's the bigger fool, you or me." She pulls me down to her and kisses me. The contact is soft at first, but urgency sets in fast.

I grasp her hips, a tentative tongue reaches out, and I open my mouth. A moan escapes me as she runs her hands up my neck and tugs at my hair.

"I want you so damn much."

We kiss again, gently at first. I run my tongue across her lips, teasing, tasting. Now Maggie groans as she arches against me.

My hands move to the buttons on her shirt, my arthritic fingers fumbling to open three of them. I spread the material and stretch my tongue out to work its way between the utilitarian white bra and her silky skin hidden within.

"Jesus."

"He's certainly not going to help." I keep applying soft kisses as I use both hands to tug the cups of her bra down, baring what I've been dreaming about all day. I suck a hardened nipple into my mouth.

"I'm not going to be able to stand much longer."

I release the hard nub and move my lips to hers as I palm her other breast, massaging the hardened tip between my fingers. She pushes against my hand, her breast filling it. I wrap one arm around her and pull her tight against me. A sensation builds low in my belly, an eruption of need.

Maggie slips her hand between us, reaches for my belt, flicks it open. The button and zipper soon follow. She pushes her hand inside, nothing barring her access. She strokes the soft curls, wiggles her hand down further, further still, dipping into warm moist folds. I open my legs. I want more. I need more.

I pull back gasping for air.

Maggie teases my entrance and then plunges two fingers into the wetness.

"Aghhhhh."

She starts rhythmically stroking me, while her thumb brushes hard against my clit.

"Mags, please." I am awash with pure sensation, desire spreading in waves. The intensity of my need makes my knees weak.

"Hold on, old girl, we're almost there."

My hips are jerking. I'm making incoherent sounds. Maggie brushes her lips against my neck and runs her tongue up my jaw. My climax teeters on the brink. She growls her satisfaction as she strokes in and out, faster, harder. Her fingers curl upward and I explode, plummeting over the edge. Sensations radiate from my toes, while a sheen of sweat coats my skin. Maggie clutches me tight with her free arm, keeping me upright.

My head drops down to her shoulder as my body continues to convulse. "Wow."

Maggie laughs softly and slowly slips from within. She runs her wet fingers up my center and wipes them across my stomach. "You earned it."

I look into her eyes, and see the love we've shared for what seems forever. "How so?"

She runs her hand down the front of my jeans and cups me.

"Well, I did leave you high and dry in the shower this morning."

I grin at the memory. "I know, but I had a very tasty treat, so it was worth running out of time."

"We almost drowned, you fool."

"Technically you can't drown in a shower."

Maggie gives me the look. It's something all wives possess the skill to use when called for. I swear it was in a manual I've never received. "Uh huh."

We turn to see the filly asleep in the hay as Moon nibbles on some oats. Maggie smiles, turns to me, and gives me a quick hug. "They're beautiful."

"Yup, but not as beautiful as you." I give her a quick kiss on the lips and pull her toward the stall across the way.

"What the hell are you doing?"

I arch my brow. "I would think that's evident." Across the aisle, I lay her down on the blanket we had spread out so many hours earlier.

"Ohh."

I open her jeans, and pull them and her panties down in one motion. "You going to scream for me tonight, Mags?"

She smiles, leaning up on her elbows. "Let's see what you've got, old woman."

I lower myself between her legs. "I can't wait to show you."

THE ADVENTURES OF A LESBIAN COWBOY

Teresa Wymore

Wherein Mr. Charlie Bluff Captures a Murderer in Rawlins and Earns the Favors of Miss Pretty Delaney.

On the wall of the stable hung coal shovels, a hayfork, and rakes. A large drill with a broken bit had a thick cobweb holding it to the wall. The brichen of a harness hung in disuse, its leather cracked and peeling. Sticks and considerable stones littered the ground near the door. My mind tried to fashion everything I saw as if I were a cobbler for feminine pleasure. Nothing seemed right. Not until I noticed the tip of a dusty milk bottle peeking from under a horse stall.

I snatched up the empty quart of Whiteman's Cream Line and wiped the open end across my shirt. The tin bail-top lid had been snapped off, and the wide glass neck was smooth.

Miss Jinny had been craning her neck to watch me, her arms braced against the stall, her cotton drawers bunched at her ankles, and her bare ass high in the air. "What do you plan to do with that, Mr. Cortland?"

After pushing her dress farther back, I rolled the bottle's texture of embossed words and rings around her skin. "I aim to screw you with it, Miss Jinny."

Her eyes roamed down my body to my trousers. "Why not use what God Almighty has given you?"

I rubbed the bulge and smiled, reluctant to confess that the Good Lord had blessed me with ambition and a steady gun hand such as proper society allows no woman. The sausage that I had planned to eat for lunch slipped down my trouser leg, so I leaned forward to distract Miss Jinny. "Or maybe you need a lickin'?"

When her eyes widened, I dropped to my knees and tongued her furry slit until she was so spent of pleasure that she lay breathless in the hay. With panting words, she asked, "How long will you be staying, Mr. Cortland?"

I set my hat on my head and adjusted the sausage. "A day. Two."

"Why then, I'd be pleased to see you again when you saddle up your horse." I stayed mum, so she added, "I'm sure I could convince Daddy to discount you a quarter for the help you gave fixing the busted stall."

I glanced at the stall she had finished nailing before I arrived. Then I winked and left.

Five years ago in Kansas City, Sealy McGuill killed my horse and used her as bait to poison wolves. But that wasn't why I was in Rawlins, although finding McGuill here and the unexpected benefit of tasting his randy daughter went a long way to paying the debt for Skinny Gin. No, I was in Rawlins because the machinists of the Union Pacific railway went to strike, and the unionists took every chance to beat the devil out of the immigrant scabs hired to replace them. Such beatings required men of low character, which is why I knew I'd find my man, Bill "Jackjaw" Bivens, in Rawlins.

The panic of '83 had scared the railway into bankruptcy, so now the high officials had to fight towns looking to make favorable contracts, corrupt politicians looking for votes, and unionists looking to start a war. The town marshal was in with the union, looking the other way whenever the anarchists took to killing scabs. Bodies had been washing up along the river for months.

That's where I came in. My name of late is "Charlie Bluff" and I work for the Pinkerton Detective Agency. I had come to the rowdy little town to get in with the unionists and find Jackjaw, who was wanted for rustling, theft, and murder.

So, after partaking of Miss Jinny's hospitality, I walked through town, where the marshal stopped me and fined me $10 for carrying a pistol. He also confiscated my Colt 45. That left me with a good story for the Capital Saloon, where I complained to anyone who would listen and went by the name of "Decker Cortland." After hurrahing it up pretty good, I put out that I had been peddling whiskey to the tribes in Alaska after working a goldmine where I was sent away for smuggling. I wanted men to get thinking I still had that swag somewhere.

A few unsavory types came sniffing around, asking questions and offering drinks. These low characters filled me in on the union bosses who had hired all manner of men for their dirty work. I set out following one of the brutes but met up with Proster Dun. He was a machinist with a wife and baby who had left the line when the union told him to, but I could tell he wasn't content to ride out the strike. When I met him outside the saloon, he was pacing.

He spit at my feet but nodded his apology and offered his name. He was nervous like a good man who wanted to do right but couldn't. He was sweating on this cool night, and blood stained his white shirt.

I eased my throat and let my voice fall from me in the deepest tone I could. "You look to have been fightin'." Despite the years I had been disguising myself as a man, it still didn't come so natural. Proster just shook his head, and I shrugged as if I didn't care beans for his conversation anyway.

We were standing on the road, and no one else was outside. The autumn night made everything like crystal, and the streets stunk of sheep. The saloon was full of mutton-punchers as well as saddle stiffs and strikers painting their tonsils and looking to dance with the saloon girls or screw the nickel-strumpets upstairs.

I wondered why Proster was outside instead of whooping it up with the rest. Part of my disguise was to go around devitalized by reverent whiskey and tobacco, like a no-account waste-it-all, so I finished rolling a cigarette, lay it on my lip, and dug for a match as if I was unsteady.

"I heard the marshal took your pistol," he said.

I lit the cigarette and swallowed the sweet smoke.

"Smells like good tobacco," he said.

"Pennsylvania by way of St. Louis," I answered.

"That where you come from?"

"There, and other places."

"Heard it said Alaska."

"Yup. But I got employ waiting on me in Texas. Lousy employ, but at least it's honest."

"Haven't had much turn with honest?"

I laughed and spit but didn't answer. He laughed back.

I breathed in deeply, enjoying the cool smoke filling my lungs. "Don't aim on going without my Colt, though. Do I look to be a scab to you?"

"Not by an acre. But no firearms in town. Didn't you see the sign?"

"Don't read." We stood staring out into the night for a while before I asked, "Know of any work? I need a room."

He scratched his cheek. "If the marshal don't like ya, best not to stick around."

"Maybe I can do him a turn, and he can give me back my Colt."

"That's up to the judge." He spit. "But I got a place you can sleep. Just for a night."

Proster led me to his house outside of town and told me I could sleep on the porch. He went into the house and returned with two blankets and said I could use a log in the yard for a pillow. I thanked him, and he went inside. As I got the log, I heard a woman's angry voice inside, followed by a baby crying. Even before this, I knew from his distraction that Proster was a man of convictions that were being tested.

As I drifted near to sleep, the door suddenly swung open, and I sat straight up, prairie dog still. I expected to see Proster, but it was his wife, Caroline, who stood at the railing staring off into the moonlight.

The night was bright enough to see her hair and eyes, and when she turned her face to me, I saw she was an angel. She had abandoned the labor of a woman's grooming, so her hair hung in a crooked black line. She had a thin mouth that bent with surmise, and her doe eyes were like something charred but still volatile. She wasn't surprised to see me there, so I believed the shouting had been about me.

"Ma'am," I said quietly, rising to my feet.

"I'm sorry to disturb you, Mr. Cortland." She didn't seem sorry. "My husband told me you needed a place to stay, and I've got no hostility to a soul in need."

"Thank you, ma'am."

She had been speaking to me as she stared out into the night, and now she turned to me squarely. "But let me assure you, if you were sent here by Mr. Bert Lloyd to keep an eye on my husband, I shall see that you're run out of this town, even if I have to do it myself."

As she spoke, her voice tight with fear but firm with resolve, I knew she would do it. I took a step toward her, unable to look away. "Mr. Lloyd is the union boss?"

Her eyes narrowed. "Everyone knows that, even a stranger in town. But no one seems to know you."

I told her my story of danger in Alaska, but she remained more suspicious than the men who had heard it.

"I'm sorry to say, Mr. Cortland," she said after a moment's thought, "but I think you're a damned liar."

Her profanity was unexpected, as was her tone. "I assure you, ma'am, I'm not here for the union. Your husband's been a chum to me."

"He's a fool, sir, as anyone can see. He doesn't have the stomach for dirty tricks, but the union put a pipe in his hand and told him to show an Irishman what it means to break a strike by breaking his bones. Now, he's in bed crying like a baby." She gazed away. "And I'm here confiding my misery to a stranger."

She had enough grit to bring a man to his knees and loins luscious enough to make it worth his while. "Who else should you confide in but someone you ain't likely to see again?" My gaze roamed around her face, and settled on her chest. Her dress, though worn, concealed ample beauties big as pumpkins. I glanced up, aware that she had caught me examining her considerables.

She moved closer, so close I could feel the warm waves of her breathing. I was tall for a woman but without the mass of the average cowboy, so I wore layers of clothing and a thick belt and vest. Still, her nearness brought me down to her size in a way no man ever had. Her eyes grew sly as she glanced about my face. I recognized that probing. She had the look of the uncanny that sometimes took hold of the more observant types who noticed my hairless lip and narrow chin.

With an easy gesture, I turned away, stepping to the railing and peering up at the moon. I rubbed my cheek, trying to impress its coarseness on her, but managing only to smear more dirt around. "I don't plan on being here long. You heard maybe I got gold stashed away, but that ain't so."

Her face went slack, her curiosity killed, so I couldn't help but intrude even more. "You seem a might much for a man like Proster Dun, pardon my say-so."

Her indifference turned to scorn. "You're not the first to notice, Mr. Cortland." She paused as if she was thinking about what she would confess before she continued. "You likely admire the saloon girls. They wear their ruffled skirts too short, but their fine petticoats are colorful and their soft kid boots have tassels, and they're all new, while you notice this cloth across my bosom is threadbare. Vulgar girls wear sequins and fringe, silk and lace, and stockings with garters—all gifts from hard luck cases like you. I'm a respectable wife, Mr. Cortland. I tend to the animals and manage the crops and make the house and have Mr. Dun's babies. And he wants more. More babies. I swear by the Good Lord's wounds, I can't handle even the two I have—the one that suckles me six times a day and the other, a grown man too frightened to beat a man who deserves it."

"And what's given you over to such a sorrowful mood, ma'am?"

"The job Mr. Dun was to perform tonight would have brought us a month's wage. Now he has no work and no money, and this shabby house will belong to the bank come month-end."

"But he did as he was told. At least the blood tells me so."

She laughed. "The blood you saw, Mr. Cortland, is my husband's own, a cut from a saw used to stop him. The man he was after got away, but not before the man's friends chased my husband back to the saloon."

I nodded at the news, just as the sound of breaking glass startled me. Several hoots of joy sounded outside as flames danced inside the window.

Caroline screamed and dashed into the house. I followed. At the cradle, she scooped up her daughter and made back for the door. I glanced about, thinking to save any valuables, but there weren't any. I hooked a burning rug on my toe and flung it out the window, but that wasn't going to stop the fire. Nothing was going to stop the rising inferno. As I started to leave, I realized Proster hadn't come from the bedroom, so I hopped over a tendril of flame and threw open the door.

Despite the smoke building like a bank of storm clouds, he was still sleeping. I rustled him from bed, and in his groggy state, he tried to hit me, but I managed to get him to the main room. The shock of fire stole the sleep from his eyes, and he shouted that we had to douse the flames. I just shook my head and shoved him through the door.

Proster stood most forlorn as he watched his life settle into ashes beneath the flames. His wife calmed the baby and then walked to the barn. Proster set to cursing God and man.

I let him stir me up, and we went to talk to the union boss, because the men who burned his house were the chums of the Irish scab he was to beat.

That's how I finally found Jackjaw, who was going by an alias and working for the anarchists. Over two bad years, he had killed three men and a woman and made off with one thousand dollars, but his luck run out the day he met me.

I played along with Proster and let him ingratiate me on Mr. Bert Lloyd, who was a bullish man with scars on his cheek. He looked to have been just as pleased to do the beating as to order it done. He took to me right away, guessing from my reputation that I was a man to be reckoned with. He said he had wired to St. Louis and Kansas City about me when I first come to town, and the Agency told him the man known as Decker Cortland was wanted for pistol-whipping a man near to death.

He offered me employ and a dollar up front. The marshal was there drinking, and he gave me back my Colt 45. Mr. Lloyd wanted me for work that very night. I figured I could get more information on the union and maybe bring Jackjaw in by myself, which meant an extra fifty dollars.

Jackjaw was a ruffian who wore a red handkerchief and black vest. He smelled of vomit and always had a hand in his trousers, adjusting his male particulars. He carried a pistol in his pocket, the barrel sticking out through a hole. Mr. Lloyd sent him to lead me and Proster to the Irishmen's hangout, which was the back room of the wire service building.

Jackjaw had two other men stand to the sides of the door and me and Proster out front. Then he tossed a smoke bomb through the window, flushing out the scabs. The unionists shot at the yowling Irish, but I backed away, keeping my shots high, acting like the smoke bothered me. When I saw Jackjaw's fearsome eyes get a bead on me, I dove behind a barrel.

Bullets splintered the wooden slats and green water soaked my trousers. I scrambled around the side of a building, seeing from the corner of my eye that Proster was laid out on the street. I wondered if Mr. Lloyd knew all along that I was a detective.

I had talked my way out of situations before, but my ambition was quarrelsome that evening, stoked by lust and disgust and sheer bad temper. All I wanted was to kill Jackjaw dead and, if it was pleasing to the Almighty, get a taste of sweet Caroline and maybe another helping of Miss Jinny before I left Rawlins.

Darkness is a chum to a man alone. I kept low and scurried around the back of the building. Keeping my pistol level, I shot at anything that moved, and that turned out to be a mongrel and one of Jackjaw's men, who fell with a gurgle. I took his gun and slipped it in my waistband as bullets hummed by my head.

A man was shooting with authority, but I couldn't find him, so I raced along the back of the building, past piles of trash and a coon, until I reached the far end. I came around the end so quickly I collided with one of the fellows. I pulled my trigger and only I got up from the ground. Another man stood trembling in front of me, but he had no gun. He was one of the Irish, and he stood shivering in his stocking feet. I nodded at him and passed by.

Before I turned the corner back into the street, I took a breath and considered how many men I might find. My work as a detective meant every day would just as likely be my last. Jackjaw wasn't worse than most, and he wasn't better, but the world would be better with him gone, even if I was gone, too.

I dashed out into the street shooting both pistols. Jackjaw was there looking the other way. He took one of my bullets in the thigh and another in his arm. He fell cursing. I kicked his pistol away but didn't finish him, though I was sorely tempted. Two remaining Irish were cowering by the door as the last ruffian made to kill them. He turned on me when I came at him like I was storming Hades, and I fired three bullets into this chest. One of his bullets caught my shoulder and spun me around, but I staggered away.

I tossed the borrowed pistol in a barrel and holstered my Colt. I didn't have a cinch for my shoulder, so I just held it as tight as I could. There was only one place I thought to go, and I don't recall making it there before I passed out.

I woke to see my angel. Caroline was smiling and dabbing my forehead. She wouldn't let me rise and told me my fever had broke that morning. The gunfight at the wire service had happened two days previous, and I was in Proster Dun's barn.

"Your husband was gunned down," I said.

She nodded without any sign of regret. "I keep expecting that no-account Mr. Bert Lloyd to send his men here for you, but no one's come. I've been living on Maggie's milk," she gestured at the cow, "and wondering what to do next."

My boss would probably keep the bonus, but I knew he would clear me of any wrongdoing. The union surely had men watching my horse, or they thought I was dead meat in the woods. I stared at Caroline, not sure what to say, until the baby cooed.

Caroline turned away to check on the girl, and when I sat up, I realized I was wearing only my drawers. In shock, I clasped my hand to my bosoms, and my look of alarm caused such a charming smile on Caroline's face that I smiled, too. The bothersome itch I had first time I saw her was back.

"I tended your troubled shoulder, Mr. Cortland." She emphasized the name. "And washed your clothes. I'm sorry to say none of Mr. Dun's survived the fire, or I would offer them to you." The humor faded from her eyes, taking even its shadow. "I don't know where I'm to go. My parents are in Boston, and they would not be pleased to see me under these circumstances."

I reached a hand to her cheek. "Why are you in such a hurry to be leaving, darlin'?" When I kissed her, she sighed and smiled nervously. She kissed me back. I watched the fear of pursuit and worry of home drain from her eyes as something more friendly took their place.

She lifted the blanket and slid in beside me. I pulled her close. We kissed until the warmth of our bodies and breath made the blanket unnecessary. She stood and tossed her dress and drawers aside, and I stared at her in utter delight. Creamy skin surrounded the bush of black fur nestled between her thighs, and her curves were robust as a new mare. Nature never made a more admirable and comely creature. I was cunt-struck worse than a cowboy after a season on the range.

I told her to turn around and bend over, and she did as she was told, spreading her sumptuous loins with immoderate haste. I got to my knees and slid my hand along her thigh. My fingers hunted their prey and the breath caught in her throat. When I finally cupped her pussy fur in my palm, I wiggled my fingers and whispered, "The man this belongs to is one lucky son of a bitch."

I couldn't see her face, but her head nodded weakly, as if she was losing her strength. "Mr. Dun," she whispered as she squatted on my palm, "never touched me so."

After rising to my feet, I bent over her and roughed up her titties as I kissed the back of her neck. "Well then, since I don't speak ill of the dead, I won't bother mentioning what a goddamn fool he was." I was no stranger to women and knew to leave gentleness for fillies that had never been broken, especially the wet-and-willing ones. I pushed her shoulders farther down until her ass was high in the air, and she reached for the wall to hold herself steady. I worked her slick hole like I was cleaning my favorite rifle, and she bobbed around like a cat rutting on a pole.

"Is this how you do a woman?" she asked, gasping every time I plunged my fingers into her. "With your hand?"

"Oh, no, darlin'. Fingering is only the beginning." I dropped on one knee and pressed my mouth to her clitchy cunt. She tasted of spring—all vital and musky, as if ready to blossom. Her ample bosoms hung low and heavy, and I pinched her nipples, which tightened into tough slugs, bullet-hard and red. When I squeezed one, I felt a trace of milk on my fingers and smeared it around.

Caroline's fertile body made my skin hungry like a morning on the trail. I kept poking and pawing her, and she was clawing leather by the time I threw off my drawers and mounted her. She lay on her back and I rode her saddle-to-saddle, my cunt kissing hers as we writhed like some unnatural beast.

She riled me with her whimpering moans, so I yanked a nipple and let it snap back. I slapped her titties around pretty good, leaving a shade of red behind, and then she started squeezing them and holding them up for me to suckle.

My steam was up and I was panting hard as I watched her fondle those fat titties, so I braced myself on both hands and rode her rough. Before blessed ecstasy could claim me, she cried loud enough to wake snakes, and then rolled her head with a howl, bucking like some feral horse. It took all my strength to bear down until her storm passed.

After she gathered her senses, she said she wanted me to cowhide her, and I was so mad with lust I wanted to, but I'd never raised a hand to a woman, even when she deserved it. I got the whip, and she settled on all fours, but I curled that strap around each of her wrists and flipped her onto her back like I'd roped a calf. She lay awkward on her bound hands, but had no complaint when I went back to nuzzling her cunt, which was soft and sweet as cherry pudding.

I was all fussed-up, so I fiddled with myself, twisting my bloated little nub until I was sloppy as a spring puddle. Caroline didn't mind my self-abuse, and began to spit out all manner of vulgar advertisements. Imagining such filthy amusements as she described sent a convulsion of bliss through me. I growled and bit at her own quivering nub, swollen again and achy for attention.

I told her it was her turn to ride, so she squatted on my face. She was pleased to grind against my nose while admonishing me for all my unnatural cravings. She ordered that I clean her shame away with my tongue and called my cuntsucking a "penance." My sweet Caroline was possessed by a foul-mouthed demon, but damned if I wasn't heated to boiling again! I licked everything she told me to, giving myself over to her tender mercies, and we didn't let up on each other until the baby cried, and then, while she nursed her daughter, I slept.

"How are we getting out of here?" she asked me as we sat at the barn door looking at the prairie later that day.

"I'm mulling that over, darlin'." I'd walked plenty of miles on my cases, sometimes hopping trains with the hobos, but I didn't reckon on a mother and baby getting far. Then again, if I turned myself in, I'd get my horse back, but I might not live long enough for the Agency to vouch for me. Not when I had information that the union boss masterminded the murders of half a dozen Irish while the marshal did nothing.

Best I could hope for was everyone thought me dead and Caroline lost in the fire. And that meant, sooner-or-later, someone would come for the bodies. As I watched Caroline tend the baby, I couldn't help but ask, "How'd a woman of such high-strung passions end up with a sorry case like Proster Dun?"

She glanced away but then squared her shoulders and stared me dead in the eye. "He was a customer at the Mikado in Santa Fe, where I went by the name of Miss Pretty Delaney."

I was indeed familiar with the Mikado. The ladies who worked that fine parlor house were known to me because of my impersonating a brothel inspector for a case three years previous.

To my most genuine surprise and appreciation, I had discovered that as long as a man was generous with his dollars, those decidedly prudent ladies didn't mind if he was, in fact, a woman.

Her defiant stare had me smiling. "Ever ride a cow?" I asked.

"As you are likely aware by now, Mr. Cortland, I've ridden many things. But never a cow."

And that's how we got halfway to Laramie before meeting up with a stage that took pity on a new mother (and kindly received the promissory note of a Pinkerton detective for eight dollars). We took a train to Kansas City, where I set up house with the new Mrs. Charlie Bluff and our baby girl.

One month later, Bill "Jackjaw" Bivens entered a land stinking of brimstone after a sudden stop at the end of a sturdy rope. Mr. Bert Lloyd escaped into the New Mexico Territory and ended his terrors on this blessed earth as the victim of a bank holdup. My parsimonious boss kept the fifty-dollar bonus, but he did buy me a drink to toast my nuptials.

PULLING

Sacchi Green

D *on't look. DON'T LOOK! Keep your eyes on the horses, the judges, anything else. Anything but the bad girl of your dreams in her fuck-me-if-you-dare outfit. Look, and you'll never be able to look away.*

But she *was* here. She'd really come. And it hadn't been just the garish lights of the midway last night; even in the noonday glare Carla smoldered, like an ember about to ignite dry leaves. The thought of stirring up that blaze made me sweat. Except it damn sure wasn't all sweat.

"She's here!" Cal said urgently. "Over by the fence!"

"Eyes front, or you're dead meat!" I snarled, just low enough not to startle the horses. The loudspeaker announcing my team drowned out my voice.

"…Ree Daniels out of Rexford, Vermont, driving Molly and Stark, with a combined weight of…"

I backed them out smoothly enough and drove briskly down the drawing ring, grip on the lines steady, attention fixed strictly on the 4,200 pounds of horsepower surging ahead of me. Two great glossy black rumps pumped in unison, two muscular bodies slowed and began their turn—and Cal stumbled on my right, just managing not to drop the evener bearing half the weight of the two single trees.

Ethan, craning to see, wavered on my left. He sped up—got into position—and the clang of the steel evener dropping onto the stoneboat's hook sent the horses lurching forward with all their strength. The heavy sledge began to move. Shoulders bunched, hocks straining, hooves the size of pie plates chopping at the dirt, they pulled a load of twice their own weight across the ground, responding to my hollered commands without really needing them until the last few feet of the required distance. Training and heart were what mattered most, not driving skill, but I still wouldn't let either of my brothers handle my team in competition.

Not that Cal hadn't given it his best shot last night. "C'mon, Ree," he'd pleaded, "she said she might come on her lunch break! And I sorta let her think I'd be driving!"

"You think she cares about anything besides the bulge in your britches?" I whapped his butt right across the wallet pocket. "You can strut your studly charms all you want tomorrow night. If you get lucky enough to have a chance at slipping something inside those tight panties of hers once the midway shuts down, you can even borrow my pickup. Tonight you get to bed all sober and early and solitary, 'cause tomorrow morning your ass is mine from dawn to whenever the pull is over and the horses rubbed down and stabled."

Cal couldn't make up his mind whether to sulk or grin. He'd have looked even younger than his eighteen years if he hadn't been six-foot-six, square-jawed, and built like somebody who'd grown up tossing around fifty-pound bales of hay. My "little" brother towered over me by four inches, which still left me six-two of height and plenty of bale-tossing capacity of my own.

I almost felt guilty at letting him get his hopes up, but I sure as hell wasn't about to tell him why.

If any slipping inside Miss Carla-from-Boston's panties was going to be done, I had a bet with myself that he wasn't going to be the one doing it. Not Cal, nor any of the other young punks—and some not so young—who hovered around her booth and pretended to be interested in throwing darts at balloons for cheesy prizes, while they watched her working her ass and tits and dark, light-my-fire eyes.

Cal and sixteen-year-old Ethan hadn't been hard to locate last night when I'd cruised the fairgrounds. Both white-blond heads, streaked hot pink and green and purple by the midway lights, loomed above the crowd. I hung back for a while near the balloon-dart booth to get an idea of what they were up to, hardly able to see the carnie huckster through the wall of testosterone-pumping adolescents between us. I could hear her slick come-on, though, and the sly, seductive tone of her voice sent hot prickles across my skin. Just food for fantasy, of course, but damn, she was good.

"C'mon folks, I'll rack 'em up again. See how Cal, here, got one right in there? Popped that cherry good? Here y'go, show us what y'got." I caught just enough movement to know she was tossing her long dark hair and twitching her hips for emphasis. "Stick that ol' dart right in! Ri-i-i-ght in there!"

"Right in where?" asked a wise guy. "Show me again!"

"If you can't find the spot on your own, hot stuff," she shot back, "maybe you better go home and practice some more on your favorite sheep."

Whoa. Considering the concentrated beer fumes in the area, she could be asking for trouble. I moved closer and squeezed in next to Cal just as the guy hurled his three darts too fast to be aiming much, and one balloon popped with a satisfying crack.

"There y'go, I knew you could hit the spot," she purred. "Prize from the first row, or wanna try again and get an upgrade?"

"How many hits to go all the way?" His leer was unmistakable.

"Sorry, Bud, my ass isn't sittin' up on the prize shelf tonight." She tossed him a big purple plush snake and moved away. "Who's next?" Her sultry gaze lit right on me, and maybe she figured it was safer not to pitch to another guy right then.

"How about you, honey? I always like to see a lady show the fellas how it's done." She put one foot up on the low barrier across the front of the booth; leaned an elbow on a sleek, black-stockinged knee; and rested her chin on her hand. The top three buttons of her red satin shirt were unbuttoned, giving me a prime view of peach-tinted flesh barely held in check by a lacy black bra. Her miniskirt was hitched up so high I caught a glimpse of matching garters and tender thighs. "How about it, darlin'?"

She sure as hell knows just how it's done! Question is, does she mean anything by it?

"Nobody here I'd call a lady," I said, looking her straight in the eye, "but I'll have a go at it anyway." I shrugged off my denim jacket and handed it to Cal, shoving him back a bit to give me room. All I wore underneath was an old white tank top smelling of sweat and horses. She handed me three darts, took my money, leaned a little farther forward, and tucked the bills loosely into her cleavage. The clueless males watching didn't seem to have any doubt that her show was for their benefit.

I raised my arm to pitch the first dart. The gaze of half the guys switched to the movement of my heavy tits—but her gaze was all that counted. And it was all I'd hoped for.

My first throw hit a red balloon, just making it bob sideways. "A real teaser, huh?" Her tone was impersonal, but a sidelong glance at my face and then my big hand hinted at more. I threw again, with a better idea of the angle required, and this time the balloon snapped and shriveled into a limp dangle of rubber. My inner tension built. When I popped the next one, too, the pressure exploding out of it seemed to pump me up right where it mattered most.

"Way to go, girl! Second shelf prize," she said. "What'll it be?"

I stifled the impulse to ask if she was still so sure her ass wasn't on that shelf. "Go on to the next guy and let me think on it a minute, okay?" I said, and she nodded, so I got down to business with my brothers. Not that I wasn't thinking on my prize real hard.

"You two go on ahead," I muttered, hauling them away. "We have to get going early tomorrow morning. Tell you what, order us all some apple crisp with ice cream down the way at that church booth, and I'll meet you there in a minute."

"Rather have some fried dough," Cal grumbled.

"Okay, whatever, anything but those damned fried onion sunburst deals!"

Cal took the money I passed him, still looking longingly back at the balloon game. Ethan looked, too, but more shyly. "Her name's Carla," Cal said. "From Boston." As if her accent, its nasal edge a notch beyond our own upcountry twang, hadn't been a give-away. "Isn't she hot? I told her about the horse pull tomorrow, and she said she likes to watch the big ones."

"I'll bet she does," I said. "Move your butts along now." And they went. Every time they do what I say I figure it may be the last, but this time I was paying them well to help with the team, so they were less inclined to argue.

When I turned back, a girl who'd been looking for her

boyfriend was making a scene at the other end of the booth. Under cover of the distraction, Carla leaned close to me. "Your brothers?" she asked, jerking her head toward Cal and Ethan's retreating asses.

"'Fraid so," I said. "You got a thing for big dumb farm boys?"

She shrugged, clearly aware that the movement made her shirt gape farther open, and that I was enjoying the view. "Not when there's a big farm girl around to distract me."

"You forgot the dumb part."

Carla looked me over slowly and thoroughly, her gaze moving down over my substantial midriff to rest on the crotch of my faded jeans.

"I'm not noticing any dumb parts," she drawled.

Damn! But attention was swinging back toward us. "So how about my prize?" I asked. "You choose for me."

She reached for a cluster of long ropes of Mardi Gras beads, slung them over my head, then swished them back and forth across my chest. My nipples responded with visible enthusiasm. "Here's a first installment," she murmured. "You gonna be around later?"

"Not tonight. Got an early wake-up call coming and a busy morning." Which wouldn't have held me back if I hadn't known Cal would come looking when I didn't show up at our RV to sleep. "Maybe tomorrow night."

"Will you be at that horse pull deal the boys were talking about?"

"Wouldn't miss it." I pulled the hank of beads off over my short pale hair and handed it back to her. "How about you hang onto these until I see you again."

A couple of customers were waving money at her by then, but Carla stuck with me for another few seconds. "Okay, but keep this one." Before I could see what she was up to, my wrists were tightly bound together by a strand of purple plastic beads. "So you won't forget."

Then she was playing to the crowd of men again, hips swaying, mouth sassing. I got my own mouth closed, stepped back into the shadows, and watched for a minute. What *was* it about her? She was good-looking but not gorgeous, and not really all that young. Which was fine with me. More than fine. What she was, was...knowing. "Hot" pretty well covered it. Hot, on the verge of bursting into flame. Something in the way she moved, as if the stroke of her clothes along her body kept her always turned on, hinted at sexual expertise country hicks at county fairs could only imagine.

I looked down at my bound wrists and imagined plenty. Breaking the fragile string would have been easy, but I wriggled loose with care, just in time to hide the beads in my pocket before Cal and Ethan came back to find me.

My imagination kept hard at work a good part of the night, too, which might have happened even if a strand of purple beads hadn't been nestled deep into the warm, wet heat between my thighs. I wasn't a dumb farm girl, not anymore, but whatever I'd got up to with girls at UMass and then in postgrad at UConn, it hadn't been much like this. I don't say that no femmes go for veterinary medicine degrees, but I sure hadn't come across anybody like Carla. The way she flaunted her body, and teased mine with her eyes; the thrust of her breasts and sway of her hips, offering and daring both at the same time... Well before dawn I had to get out of the RV and find a place to do some serious solitary teasing and thrusting of my own, and even that only slowed me down to a simmer.

In the morning the horses got me back on focus. Molly and Stark had been pulling in competitions all summer and knew what was what. They were about as psyched up as Percherons

get, and maybe more than most. The huge black horses have
been bred for double-muscling for centuries, but they have spirit
and heart as well.

By noon they'd come through the first few elimination
rounds and hardly broken a sweat. This last load had been
more of a challenge, but they'd handled it well. There were
only four teams left in competition, and two of them I knew
we couldn't beat without straining hard enough to risk injury.
My pair were relatively young, full-grown but without all the
heft a few more years would give them, and Molly would never
quite achieve the muscle mass her brother could. Letting a mare
pull was, in fact, pretty rare. I got a lot of flak from old-timers
for it, but she had the spirit, and I'd decided to give her one
more year before breeding her and complicating her life with
motherhood.

I watched the loader piling another 1,500 pounds of concrete
blocks on the stoneboat. So far I'd never set the team at a weight
I wasn't sure they could handle. Should I drop out at this stage
and settle for an honorable fourth? Would I quit now, if I didn't
want so badly to impress somebody who was watching?

Hell no! Molly nudged me hard with her big velvety nose and
blew as though in agreement. I whacked her shoulder compan-
ionably, turning my head a few degrees—and there was Carla
right in my line of sight. Her mouth hung open, and her eyes
were wide with something that might have been fear. I grinned
and nodded. Her usual cock-sure, seductive expression took
over again right away, but she still eyed Molly warily.

Then Cal waved and called to her, and I had to whack *his*
shoulder to get him back on task. The first team of this round
was trotting toward the loaded sledge. I was sure these huge
Belgians were up to the weight, but their driver's helpers didn't
get a secure hook before the horses bolted forward, and missed

on the second try, too, so that by the time they did get a good hook the team was too flustered to pull together. I elbowed Cal meaningfully in the ribs.

The second team gave it a good try, but stopped a few feet short in spite of all their driver's yelling. Then we were up. I bent for one last feel of each horse's hocks to be sure there was no tenderness, straightened from between enormous equine legs— and the quick flash of horrified awe in Carla's eyes sent a jolt of power crackling through my cunt.

Wow! But...no time for that now. No time for anything beyond keeping control of the eager horses while Cal and Ethan hustled to drop the evener onto the hook, and then the team's surge of power when I sent the order through the lines. The loaded stoneboat moved, caught, moved again, slid a few feet, slowed—"Hup! Hup! Hup!" I hurled my voice at them like an extra ton of muscle, of breath, of heart, and they took it all and gave back more, struggling onward just because they refused to stop. And then the judge signaled that they'd made the distance, and the boys released the sled.

My gorgeous pair of black, sweat-flecked treasures pranced back to the far end of the arena, proud, hyped by the applause, and, I knew from their gait, just slightly sore from the strain on their hocks.

After the last team made its distance, I waved off the next round. Second place was fine for now. Molly and Stark would give me everything they had, but I didn't need to make them find their limit at the risk of injury.

When the event was over and the rosettes awarded, I drove them into the warm sunshine, keeping an eye out for Carla. Cal and Ethan had been headed off by a gaggle of cheerleader chicks, just the types that always give me flashbacks to the horrors of high school. The boys were welcome to 'em.

There she was, keeping a safe distance. "That was...some-thing." Words uncharacteristically failed her.

"Sure was," I agreed. "I need to get them rubbed down now and tape their legs. Want to come along and make their closer acquaintance?"

"I have to get back...I'm late already...but I close down tonight at 10." Molly's inquisitive black head swung toward her. Carla stepped back in a hurry.

"Then 10 is when I'll be there," I said, riding a wave of confidence.

Carla tried for a note of command. "You'd better be." She turned away, her fine ass eloquent with an assumption of power. But I'd seen some cracks in her eat-my-attitude self-possession, some fear and awe, maybe even excitement. And I'd enjoyed the hell out of how it made me feel. Those beads tight around my wrists—well, they'd sure sparked a tingle of anticipation and curiosity, and there was no denying that I'd go along with a lot just for the promise of some hot, wet, sweaty sex. Still, power was such a rush...It was going to be an interesting night, to say the least.

I was there, in fact, at 8, and again at 9, just passing by, in range of her voice but not in her line of sight. Cal caught up with me in the next row at 9:30 and groused that Carla had turned him down. "She's prowling around like a cat in heat, but says she's got other plans, and that's that. Didn't exactly tell me to fuck off, but close enough."

"You can still borrow my pickup," I said generously. "I'll probably just keep an eye on the horses tonight in the barn. What about those girls who've been trailing you around all day? I saw a couple of 'em hanging with Ethan over by the Tilt-a-Whirl." He shrugged, but grabbed my keys fast enough and took off toward the rides with a fair show of enthusiasm. Good thing he was too full of what filled his own pants to notice how his big sister was prowling around.

At 10 sharp Carla was shooing the last few customers away. I stepped up, unlatched the front canvas flap, and started to lower it. "Closing time, sport," I said to the last reluctant straggler. He started to object, tilted back his head to look up at me, paused reflexively at my chest, finally saw my expression, and decided he had business elsewhere. I dropped the flap to close us in and stepped over the low barrier—and into a role I was making up as I went along.

Her back was turned while she unclipped balloon fragments from the backboard. She'd shot me a little smile when I arrived, but there was something tentative about it, wary. Or maybe even nervous. I kind of liked the idea of making her nervous.

"So what does it take," I asked, pressing right up against her ass and putting my hands on her hips, "for a big old farm girl to distract you?"

She turned right around into my arms and did a slow grind against me. "It's been a while since I got that lucky," she said against my chin. "What do you generally have in mind when you pick up slutty carnival hucksters?"

"Once I pick 'em up," I said, digging my hands into her round asscheeks and raising her so that her breasts rested above mine, "my mind doesn't have all that much to do with it." Which was pretty much true. "But I've been known to offer to buy a girl dinner. To keep her strength up."

She grabbed onto my shoulders and pushed herself higher. My nose was right in her cleavage, and her musky scent telegraphed messages all the way down to my dampening cunt. "If you're hungry," she teased, "I have better ideas. If you think you can keep your strength up."

Well, I had better ideas, too. Like digging my teeth into the lace of her bra where it peeked through her unbuttoned shirt, and tugging. One nipple was about to pop free from constraint. "Hungry" didn't begin to describe it.

"But not here," she said, digging her knees hard into my midriff and straining away. I whoofed, groaned a complaint, and let her slide gradually down. One bent knee ground deliberately into my crotch as it went past, forcing out a different tone of groan.

"Think of the show we're putting on for anybody watching our shadows through the canvas," she said, once her feet were on the ground.

"We could just turn the damned light off," I said. "Or, what the hell, sell tickets to the show."

Carla scooped up a handful of the metal clamps that had held balloons to the wires strung along the backboard. "Nope." But she did turn out the light. "For what I have in mind, we'd knock the whole booth over, if you're as strong as you think you are."

That got my attention all right. So did the clamps. "So where are we going?" All I had to offer was a few not-so-clean blankets in a horse trailer, or a bunk in an RV that might fill up with randy teenagers at any moment. *Smooth. Really smooth, Casanova.*

"To my cheap, tacky motel room. Where else?" She edged through the canvas flap into the night still bright with streaks of garish colored light from the rides, and throbbing with the heavy beat of music. I followed, choosing strong-and-silent over the distinct possibility of making a fool of myself.

Her car was battered and dented. Prying open the passenger side door might have been a test of strength in itself, but, if so, I passed. Carla's skirt was hitched up so high in the driver's seat that I didn't refuse the invitation to explore beyond her garters, in the process making sure I'd know how to either unhook them with one hand when the time seemed right, or to work right past them. I couldn't recall anyone at vet school ever wearing garters.

From the pungent wetness of my fingers when we reached the motel, I knew Carla'd been more distracted than any driver should be, but when I tried to clinch just inside the door she pushed me away. "My room, my rules," she said sternly.

"We'll see," I said, leaning back against the closed door. Skin flushed, lips full and moist, heat practically radiating from her thighs, Carla clearly wanted it as much as I did. "What've you got in mind? Something like 'The bigger they come, the harder they fall'?"

"And the harder they come," she said, her purr verging on a growl. "Get on the bed."

Well, what else was I here for? I strode over, trying to look like it was my own idea. Then I saw what was fastened to the metal posts of the bed. "Wait a minute, aren't those the strings of beads I won?"

She reached into her purse. "Plenty more where those came from." Her voice became a falsetto caricature of a Mardi Gras reveler. "Hey, baby, show me your tits and I'll throw you some beads!"

I laughed and shrugged out of my jacket, making sure the small tin of horse lube from my vet kit didn't fall out of its pocket. Then I plopped down on the bed. "Show you my tits? If you can't find 'em on your own, baby, maybe you better go back and practice on your balloons."

She launched herself forward. I was flat on my back, jeans unzipped and yanked down past my ass, shirt pulled way up and nipples firmly twisted between her fingers, before I could do more than grunt.

"Spread 'em," she ordered, kneeing me without mercy. "Arms too." She let go of my tits to push my hands toward the corners of the bed, which of course let her tempting breasts hang right above my mouth.

I went along with it. "You're going to tie me with just those flimsy strings of beads?"

"That's the plan." She got right to it. "Sure, you're thinking you can break free any time. But if you do, you lose out. The challenge is to hold still, no matter what I do to you." She reversed direction to work on tying my ankles. Now her crotch, skirt pushed up to her hips, was right above my face. So much for getting into her panties; she wasn't wearing any. I breathed in her scent hungrily but didn't try to arch up toward her. I definitely didn't want to lose out.

So I lay still, if not silent, when the clamps came out. She moved them along my flesh like crab claws traveling across a dune, digging into my belly, my ribs, the lower swell of my breasts. Anticipation became as sharp as sensation, until my nipples seemed to be straining toward the promise of pain. When the metal bit into my tender peaks with cold fire, my stifled scream had as much of relief in it as anguish.

My shoulders clenched, my chest heaved, but I managed to keep my arms and legs nearly still. Carla watched my face, and bent to chew my lips when they twisted with the effort to be silent.

"Not bad," she muttered against my mouth, "for starters." Her tongue nudged at my gritted teeth until I relaxed them and let her probe deeply. The sheet under my hips grew hot and damp as I imagined that supple tongue probing elsewhere.

Carla finally reared back and released the clamps. Pain flooded back into areas that had become nearly numb. Then I felt the procession of crab pinches travel up my inner thighs.

"How're we doing?" she asked cheerfully, bending her head to watch her handiwork.

"Next time," I gasped, "how about a room with a mirror on the ceiling?" Her head was dipping lower. Was that brief pinch on my pussy lips from metal, or fingers? And was that... oh, God! Hot, wet, thrusting deep and deeper, her face hidden between my thighs... My hips arched, my cunt grasped at the pressure, but Carla's tongue retreated, flicking my clit enough to swell it to desperation, but not quite to ignition.

"Don't move!" she said, and kept at me, teasing with darting tongue and pinching fingers until my throat was raw with groans and curses. But I must not have moved hard enough to break the strings of beads, because they still hadn't snapped.

Until suddenly she pressed harder, and deeper, hands under my ass pushing me upward toward the mouth that gave me everything I wanted, everything I could take. My wrists and ankles tore free as I forgot everything but the fierce, consuming bite of orgasm.

"Is that what you call losing out?" I said faintly, when I got enough breath back.

"You did okay," Carla said. "Look at your wrists."

They were scraped and bleeding, and so were my ankles. The damned strands of beads hadn't been so easy to break after all. "Looks like...looks like I didn't meet your challenge as well as I thought."

She shrugged. "Those suckers are tougher then you'd think. Nylon string, knots between each bead. There's a fastener on each necklace that just pops open, but once you release that and tie 'em like rope they're really strong. Don't go thinking something's flimsy just because it looks tacky and flashy and cheap."

"I don't see anything here tacky and flashy and cheap," I said.

Carla leaned back and spread her thighs. The garters and belt had disappeared somewhere along the line.

"Show me what you got, then, big girl," she said, "and tomorrow I'll meet any challenge you name. Even if it means getting up close and personal with horses as big as elephants and twice as mean."

So I did, with hands that were hard where she was softest, leaving bruises to be savored for days. Finally, my fingers slicked with the horse lube, I worked my way deep into the first cunt I'd known that could swallow me to the wrist and clamp hard enough to give me bruises of my own. Not that I noticed those until much later, or the marks of her nails on my shoulders.

And Carla did meet her own challenge. Molly's broad black back will never look more glorious than it did when a dark-haired, seductive, naked Lady Godiva rode her through the horse barns one unforgettable midnight at the county fair.

ABOUT THE AUTHORS

JOVE BELLE lives in Portland, Oregon. Her novels include *Edge of Darkness* and *Split the Aces*, both from Bold Strokes Books, and the forthcoming *Chaps*.

CHEYENNE BLUE moves between Australia, Ireland, and Colorado. Her stories have appeared in many anthologies, including *Best Women's Erotica*; *Best Lesbian Love Stories*; *Rode Hard, Put Away Wet*; and *Mammoth Book of Lesbian Erotica*.

ANDREA DALE's (cyvarwydd.com) stories have appeared in *Where the Girls Are*, *Best Lesbian Romance*, *Best Lesbian Love Stories*, and *Crossdressing: Erotic Stories*, among many others. She is the coauthor of the novels *A Little Night Music* and *Cat Scratch Fever*, forthcoming from, respectively, Cheek Books and Black Lace Books.

CHARLOTTE DARE's (myspace.com/charlotte_dare) erotic fiction has appeared in *Tales of Travelrotica for Lesbians, Vol. 2;*

Ultimate Lesbian Erotica 2008 / 2009; Wetter; Purple Panties; Island Girls; and *Where the Girls Are: Urban Lesbian Erotica.* She also has work forthcoming in the anthology *Girl Crazy.*

DEJAY (dejaynovl@gmail.com) lives six months of the year in the mountains of Pennsylvania. Two of her short stories, "Who's in Charge" and "Silent Journey," can be found in the October 2008 issue of *Khimairal Ink.*

DELILAH DEVLIN (delilahdevlin.com) is the author of *Down in Texas, Jane's Wild Weekend,* the *Dark Realm* series, and many other books and stories. Her books have won numerous awards, including an Eppie for Best Erotic Romance Science Fiction (*Shadow Warrior*).

ROXY KATT (roxykatt.com & roxykatt.blogspot.com) lives in Canada. Her work has appeared in *Where the Girls Are; Erotika: Bedtime Stories; The Mammoth Book of Lesbian Erotica; Best Lesbian Erotica 2008;* and other collections.

RADCLYFFE is a retired surgeon and author-publisher with more than thirty lesbian novels and anthologies in print. Two of her books, *Erotic Interludes 2: Stolen Moments* (ed. with Stacia Seaman) and *Distant Shores, Silent Thunder,* have won the Lambda Literary Award. She has stories in *Best Lesbian Erotica 2006, 2007, 2008,* and *2009* and is the editor of *Best Lesbian Romance 2009* and *2010* (Cleis Press). She is also the president of Bold Strokes Books, an independent LGBTQ publishing company.

JEAN ROBERTA (JeanRoberta.com) teaches English in a Canadian prairie university and writes in various genres. Her erotic stories have appeared in more than 60 print anthologies, including seven editions of the annual *Best Lesbian Erotica* series and her single-author collection, *Obsession* (Eternal Press). She writes reviews for the website eroticarevealed.com and a monthly column, "Sex is All Metaphors," for erotica-readers.com.

CRAIG J. SORENSEN has published stories in anthologies edited by Alison Tyler (*Hurts So Good, Frenzy, Afternoon Delights*), Rachel Kramer Bussel (*Tasting Her, Tasting Him*), and online at various sites including *Clean Sheets*.

CECILIA TAN (ceciliatan.com) is the author of numerous books of erotica including *White Flames* (Running Press), *Black Feathers* (HarperCollins), and *The Velderet* (Circlet Press.) Susie Bright calls her "simply one of the most important writers, editors, and innovators in contemporary American erotic literature." She is founder and editor of Circlet Press, Inc. and also writes and edits for Ravenous Romance and many other publishers.

ELAZARUS WILLS is an artist, used bookstore owner, journalist, and writer of erotic romantic fiction living in a small mountain town in Colorado. His work has appeared in several recent gay-themed print anthologies, including Simon Sheppard's *Leathermen,* as well as being regularly featured in the online erotic fiction magazine *Ruthie's Club*.

TERESA WYMORE (teresawymore.com) is the author of the erotic fantasy *Darklaw* and other books. Her fiction has appeared in such anthologies as *Cream: The Best of the Erotica Readers and Writers Association* and *Wild Nights: (Mostly) True Stories of Women Loving Women*.

ABOUT THE EDITORS

RAKELLE VALENCIA is an equine behavior and language clinician teaching throughout the country. She has worked with more than one thousand horses of all breeds and disciplines in gentling or restarting. Roping and riding have been lifeskills, played out in both her passions of working with horses and erotic writing. Rakelle has co-edited five erotic anthologies, most recently *Lipstick on Her Collar* (Pretty Things Press). Her first, *Rode Hard, Put Away Wet* (Suspect Thoughts Press), was a finalist for a Lambda Literary Award. The author of many erotic short stories, she has also published technical articles on the subject of Natural Horsemanship.

SACCHI GREEN lives in western Massachusetts and New Hampshire. Her stories have appeared in many collections, including seven volumes of *Best Lesbian Erotica*, four of *Best Women's Erotica*, *Best Lesbian Romance*, and *Penthouse*. With Rakelle Valencia, she has co-edited three lesbian erotica anthologies: *Rode Hard, Put Away Wet* (Suspect Thoughts Press); *Hard Road, Easy Riding* (Haworth Press, reissued by Lethe Press); and *Lipstick on Her Collar* (Pretty Things Press). She's also the editor of the recent anthology *Girl Crazy* from Cleis Press.